A MURDER ON LONDON BRIDGE

THE KITTY WORTHINGTON MYSTERIES, BOOK 13

MAGDA ALEXANDER

HEARTS AFIRE PUBLISHING

CHAPTER 1

LONDON 1925

SUPPER AT LORD AND LADY RUTLEDGE'S

It was with a great deal of pride that Robert and I welcomed our guests to our first formal dinner as husband and wife. To tell the truth, it should have happened months ago. But the death of Robert's brother had precluded an earlier celebration.

His absence was keenly felt by our family, especially Mother and Father, who'd been his closest friends. But the one who'd missed him most was Robert, as he'd been Robert's mentor long before he discovered they were related. Not only related, but the heir to the Rutledge title and everything that went along with it.

With the assumption of the title came certain responsibilities, one of which being we had to be social. With time marching on, Robert had decided April was the right time to hold our first formal dinner party. Having learned from the best, Mother, I was infinitely familiar with what that entailed. Scrumptious food, gorgeous place settings, and, of course, a guest list that included the familiar and the new.

My parents, naturally, were there. And so were my brothers, Richard and Ned; Lady Lily, Ned's fiancée; Lady Emma, who would soon become Lady Marlowe; and Marlowe himself. Lady Mellie, our newest Assistant Lady Detective, as well as our dear friend, Hollingsworth's sister, was present as well. Sadly, he was still on his travels. Last we heard, he'd landed in Greece. We sorely missed his presence and hoped he would soon return to us.

Last, but not least, we'd invited Mister Merton, an antiquities dealer, and his wife. One might think Merton an odd person to invite to our first formal dinner, as he was neither related nor a close friend. But Robert thought he would be an interesting dinner guest. I had to agree. During a sudden rainstorm, Robert had sought shelter in his shop. Given his love of rare books, he'd become fascinated by what he'd discovered there. So, of course, we'd extended the invitation, which Merton was not slow to accept.

As our guests arrived, we welcomed them in our drawing room, where a cheerful fire glowed in the grate. A footman moved with practiced ease, offering flutes of champagne and glasses of sherry. Conversation flowed easily among family and friends. The Mertons were soon included as they were drawn in with gentle encouragement.

With the evening happily established, I decided it was time to satisfy my curiosity about Lily's wedding plans. She looked radiant beneath the candlelight, the glow catching in her blonde hair and the subtle shimmer of pearls at her throat.

Joining her by the hearth, I lowered my voice just enough to carve out a private moment amid the broader din. "So," I said, "how are the wedding plans coming along?"

Lily's eyes sparkled as she laughed. "Everything's

proceeding exactly according to plan. Down to the last embroidered napkin."

"I should have known," I teased.

"Mother Worthington has been . . . wonderfully involved."

"Mother Worthington?" I echoed, lifting a brow.

Lily flushed ever so slightly, though she looked pleased. "It felt natural, somehow. She's been incredibly kind and rather determined to make this wedding a triumph."

"Oh, I've no doubt of that," I said. "Has she introduced you to 'The File Folders' yet?"

Lily laughed again. "Oh yes. Each one neatly labeled, color-coded, and cross-referenced. One for flowers, one for food, one for the guest list, one for music. There's even one labeled *Possible Weather Contingencies*."

"That sounds exactly like Mother," I said with a grin. "She created a folder labeled *Kitty's Future* when I was fourteen. It included a list of eligible peers and my ideal hairstyle."

"She only wants everything to be perfect," Lily said gently. "And honestly, I rather love the folders. I've always liked a bit of order amidst the chaos."

"I suppose they do have a certain charm," I conceded. "Like a military campaign in paper form."

"Exactly," Lily agreed.

"Well, I'm relieved to hear the bride hasn't been buried beneath fabric swatches or kidnapped by a runaway florist."

"Not yet," she said. "Though I've heard the cake designer has opinions."

I placed a hand to my heart. "Ah, yes, the Cake Wars. No one escapes unscathed."

Lily beamed. "I'm so glad you'll be by my side as an attendant, not just as my soon-to-be sister, but my friend."

"Always," I said, and meant it.

She reached for my hand and gave it a small squeeze, and for a moment, the world felt perfectly splendid.

The laughter grew brighter, the glasses clinked, and by the time we were summoned to the dining room, the evening already felt like a success.

Our dining room positively glowed under the candlelight, all soft shadows and golden flickers. Polished mahogany, gleaming crystal, and china so fine I was almost afraid to touch it.

As Lady Rutledge—I was still getting used to that title—I sat at one end of the table while Robert—as Lord Rutledge—sat at the head. We began with a spring pea and watercress soup, the color so vivid it looked as though someone had dipped a brush straight into a meadow. A touch of mint gave it an unexpected brightness—refreshing, though I rather missed the comfort of something with a little more body. Still, it seemed to please everyone.

The pheasant, of course, was the centerpiece—and quite right, too. Roasted to golden perfection and brushed with a whisper of lavender-honey glaze, it was the sort of dish that practically announced, *"You're dining at Rutledge House now, darling. Do try to keep up."* As if either Robert or I cared about such pomp. Cook had tested the lavender idea three times before settling on the precise measure. Leave it to her to make a bird smell faintly of an herb garden and somehow still taste like heaven.

The new potatoes glistened with chive butter, and the asparagus was braised until just the right amount of tender, with a lemony bite that made one feel terribly virtuous. The baby carrots, too, sweet and caramelized, added just enough cheer to balance the rest.

I didn't pretend to be a connoisseur of wine, though I'd tasted enough at society dinners to spot the difference between something truly excellent and something merely expensive. The white Burgundy served with the pheasant that evening was, happily, both.

Before long, Mother dabbed at the corners of her mouth with her napkin, her eyes sparkling with thinly veiled anticipation. "Everyone," she said, her voice slicing cleanly through the clink of silver and low hum of conversation, "Richard has something he'd like to share."

I set down my wine glass, looking fondly at my brother across the table. Robert tipped his head in quiet encouragement.

"Thank you, Mother," Richard began with a small, modest smile. "As some of you may recall, I'd mentioned that I would be lecturing at Oxford over the summer. Well,"—he let the words hang just long enough to catch our attention—"after further discussions, the university has decided to bring me in earlier than planned. I'll be teaching during Trinity term."

"So you'll start in two weeks?" Emma asked.

"That's the plan. I'll be focusing on archaeology—particularly my fieldwork in Egypt—as well as the ancient trade routes that connected Egypt, Greece, and the Near East."

A ripple of polite surprise traveled around the table, followed by soft applause. I couldn't help beaming. "Oh, Richard, how wonderful! You must be thrilled."

"I am," he said warmly, his eyes meeting mine for a heartbeat. "It's a rare chance to combine excavation work and historical interpretation. I'm rather looking forward to it."

Mother gave a prim, satisfied little nod, as though she had personally orchestrated the whole affair, which, to tell the truth, I wouldn't put past her. She'd do anything to keep Richard home.

Robert raised his glass with a wry half-smile. "To Richard. May his students find him as fascinating as we do."

Laughter rippled softly through the room, the clink of crystal and silver wrapping the moment in gentle warmth as we toasted to Richard's new chapter.

Mr. Merton gave an approving nod. "A fine topic, young

man. One can learn much about a people by the objects they leave behind. That's always fascinated me."

"As it should," Richard said, warming to the subject. "Trade is civilization in many ways. It reveals everything—what a society valued, feared, worshipped. The everyday and the sacred all wrapped up in grain shipments and pottery fragments."

"And if the lectures go well?" Lord Marlowe prompted.

"A permanent position in the autumn," Richard admitted, trying—unsuccessfully—not to beam. "A lecturer's post, if the department finds my lectures satisfactory."

"Which I'm sure they will," I said confidently. "You've a knack for making dusty things seem rather compelling."

"It's splendid news, Richard," Father added, a rare softness in his voice. "We're quite pleased."

I could see why he felt that way. It would mean Richard would remain in England, at least for a time. As Richard suffered from malaria, he could never return to his archaeological digs in Egypt. To do so would mean a likely death if he suffered a relapse.

I was proud of my brother—his brilliance, his steadiness. And more than a little relieved he'd be staying on home soil. "Will you be residing with Margaret and Sebastian while in Oxford?" I asked.

"They have issued an invitation which I'm more than glad to accept. Their house is a darn sight better than a leased flat." Sebastian had bought a house at Norham Gardens, one of the more exclusive Oxford neighborhoods, for those times when he and my sister Margaret resided there. As chair of a committee to increase women's enrollment at the university, her efforts had already shown progress, but it was early days yet. She also had raised funds to establish a women's health clinic and had been highly successful in that effort. Sebastian hadn't been idle. He'd been instrumental in an effort to increase organic farming in the United Kingdom.

With the birth of baby Thomas, those efforts had been put temporarily on hold as they both wanted to enjoy time with their child. They planned to resume their efforts during the summer, which meant Richard would have the house to himself, at least during Trinity term.

"I must say, Lady Rutledge," Mr. Merton said, dabbing delicately at his mouth with a linen napkin, "this is a most delicious meal. Your cook has outdone herself."

"Indeed," his wife added with a polished smile. "The pheasant is exquisite."

"Thank you," I said, returning the smile. "Cook takes great pride in her work. Deservedly so."

When the conversation lagged, Robert said, "Mr. Merton is something of an expert in antiquities."

The gentleman chuckled. "Expert may be generous, Lord Rutledge, but I do have a fondness for lost manuscripts and forgotten relics."

Richard perked up. "Manuscripts? Truly?"

"Indeed," Merton said. "Letters, old books, particularly those presumed lost during key moments in history."

"Any discoveries of late?"

Merton hesitated—just enough to make us all lean in—then smiled as if letting us in on a delicious secret. "As a matter of fact, yes. Though I hesitate to say too much just yet."

"You can't leave us hanging, sir," Marlowe said, grinning. "We're utterly captivated."

"Well, then," Merton said, eyes glinting, "but only among friends. I've recently acquired a manuscript—quite rare, possibly quite significant."

"A manuscript?" Richard leaned forward.

"London. 1666," Merton said, lowering his voice.

The effect was immediate. The room quieted, and even the candle flames seemed to still.

"The year of the Great Fire?" Emma whispered.

Merton nodded solemnly. "I believe this document contains an account not found in the known records."

"What sort of account?" I asked, intrigued despite myself.

He smiled. "That, Lady Rutledge, is what I am in the process of verifying. But if I'm right, it may reveal truths long buried."

Robert's tone turned measured. "And does it mention anyone by name?"

"Ah," Merton said, with maddening vagueness. "That is the very question, isn't it? But let's not get ahead of ourselves. More soon, I hope."

A chill tickled down my spine—not cold exactly, but a curious, quiet knowing. There was something in his tone. Something in the way he spoke of the past like it still had power to strike.

But I refused to be concerned about something that might not come to pass. Not during our glorious dinner. "Shall we make our way to the drawing room? We can enjoy our dessert there, along with coffee and tea."

Once we assembled there, the conversation drifted. Talk of the spring season. A new comedy on the West End. A scandal involving an heiress, a poet, and a mislaid engagement ring. But I couldn't quite shake the feeling Merton's words had stirred.

Before too long, our guests made their farewells, each offering effusive praise and warm gratitude for the lovely meal. As the door clicked shut behind the last departing guest, Robert lingered beside me, his gaze soft as it swept over the candlelit room.

"That was a splendid dinner," he said quietly. "Everything was just right—the food, the company, the atmosphere. And you, Catherine..." He brushed a curl from my cheek. "You were the heart of it all."

I tilted my head, eyes dancing. "Flattery will get you ... anything you want, My Lord."

His smile curved slow and warm. "Is that so?" He leaned down and kissed me—lightly, teasingly, a brush of lips that still managed to leave me breathless. When he pulled back, his thumb traced a small circle at my wrist.

"Splendid as the evening was, however, I sense you're troubled," his voice quiet but certain.

Not a surprise he'd correctly assessed my mood. He'd always been able to read me like a book.

"Merton's manuscript. It unsettles me."

His eyes met mine. "It unsettles me, too. There's something about the way he phrased it."

I nodded. "Would it be too inquisitive of me to find out more?"

A faint smile curved his lips. "Would it stop you if I said yes?"

"Not in the least," I said, grinning.

"Then by all means," he said. "Pay Mr. Merton a visit."

Though I hadn't yet named it aloud, a quiet certainty stirred within me. Whatever truths lay hidden in that manuscript, they weren't merely historical. They were dangerous.

CHAPTER 2

LADIES OF DISTINCTION DETECTIVE AGENCY

The morning after our wonderful supper, I arrived at the Ladies of Distinction Detective Agency to find it buzzing with energy, a sign of the insanity unfolding around us. Our office was being readied for our big move.

With three full-fledged lady detectives, one full-time gentleman detective, one assistant lady detective, a new gentleman detective, a bookkeeper, and a receptionist, our current space had grown increasingly cramped. To accommodate our growing needs, we'd recently signed a lease on a stunning four-story Georgian terrace on Essex Street, conveniently close to the Underground and the Middle Temple barristers. The larger space wouldn't just allow us to work more comfortably. It would lend an added air of legitimacy to our already well-respected agency.

But, as with all good things, there was a price to pay. The move date—just a week away—meant that alongside our usual busy caseload, workmen were bustling in and out, packing and preparing. Needless to say, at the moment, it was utter bedlam.

Boxes were piled like miniature cityscapes around Emma's office, their labels hastily scrawled in thick black pencil: *Case Files – Confidential*, *Surveillance Equipment*, *Tea Things – Fragile*. One had already begun to lean drunkenly to one side, rescued only by a nearby chair leg. Movers tramped in and out with the solemnity of undertakers and the clumsiness of overgrown puppies.

Despite it all, Emma remained serenely poised behind her desk—what little remained of it. The blotter had vanished, the lamp unplugged, and someone had packed away the inkwell. Only her elegant fountain pen and a teetering stack of folders kept her command post from looking entirely deserted.

I sat across from her—on the edge of a chair that had clearly been earmarked for wrapping, judging by the twine coiled beneath it. Somewhere down the corridor, something made of glass shattered. No one screamed, which I took as a good sign.

Emma tapped a folder with one perfectly manicured finger. "The Harwood case. Allegations of a missing will. Touchy family dynamics. Best if you handle it."

I nodded, taking it from her. "And you're still following up on the Langford affair?"

"Yes. A question of forged paintings and a very self-important baronet who insists he knows better than an expert's analysis. I've half a mind to let him be swindled, just to teach him humility."

We both smiled, then turned as a loud thud shook the doorframe. One of the movers muttered something apologetic and edged back out with a framed photograph tucked under his arm.

"I've asked Mr. Clapham to handle that criminal matter

from Sir Frederick," Emma continued. "Something to do with a forged trust deed—maybe criminal, maybe civil. Given his experience as a detective inspector at Scotland Yard, he's best equipped to sort that tangle."

"He does seem to thrive when something borderline illegal crops up," I said fondly. "Like a bloodhound with a whiff of scandal."

Emma didn't disagree. "Aurelia, as always, is up to her elbows in infidelity inquiries."

"She has an uncanny gift for spotting lipstick on collars and lies on lips," I agreed. "Sometimes I wonder if she wasn't secretly married to a rake in a past life."

"She'd have frightened the poor man into virtue," Emma said lightly.

"What about Major Lane?" I asked. We'd brought him on to handle the sorts of cases best left to a man—particularly those involving gentlemen's clubs and private dealings where a lady's presence might raise eyebrows.

"He's working with Colonel Fairleigh," Emma replied, flipping to the relevant page in her notes. "Retired cavalry. Apparently, a substantial amount of brandy and a set of antique dueling pistols have gone missing from his study. He refuses to believe his son took them and insists someone's trying to undermine his honor."

I stifled a smile. "Let me guess. He wanted someone he could talk to man-to-man?"

Emma's lips twitched. "Naturally. And Major Lane knows exactly how to salute and nod in all the right places."

I arched a brow. "Just don't ask him to dance. He claims it's against his principles and possibly his sense of balance."

Emma chuckled, then flipped to the next page in her notes. "Now, as for Mellie, I've assigned her to assist both Aurelia and Clapham this week, depending on who needs the extra hands. She's improving steadily, but she's not quite ready to take on clients of her own."

"She's enthusiastic, if nothing else," I said, glancing toward the window, where I could see Mellie across the courtyard, talking with a vaguely familiar lady. "We all have to start somewhere."

Emma nodded and glanced around at the semi-packed room. "Yes, well. We'll survive the move—somehow. In a week, the new offices will be up and running. Until then, we'll continue operating amid boxes, confusion, and the occasional furniture mishap."

Another crash echoed down the hall.

Emma didn't even flinch. "That, I believe, was the umbrella stand."

Mellie poked her head into the room. "Another case just came in—a missing bracelet from Lady Dorsett. She believes one of her guests pocketed it at her last soirée."

I sighed. "Another theft case. Valuables are disappearing rather frequently all across London."

Emma stacked the files neatly. "That makes for six new cases just this week."

"You want me to handle it?" Mellie's eagerness was breathtaking. When Emma and I hesitated, she added, "I know her. She attended my debut ball."

"Does she have any idea who took it?" Emma asked.

"Lady Petersham. They were in the withdrawing room at the same time. Lady Dorsett removed the bracelet to wash her hands. Next thing she knew, it was gone."

"Well, that seems to point in a certain direction," I said.

"Lady Petersham has been known for 'borrowing' things," Mellie said. "She needs to be approached in a particular way, that's all."

"Sounds like you have a perfect understanding of the situation." I glanced at Emma, who nodded her consent. "Investigate away, Mellie."

"Don't forget to collect a retainer," Emma reminded her.

"Shall we say fifty pounds?" Mellie asked.

"That's rather rich," I said, gazing at Emma. "Don't you think?"

"Our services are worth it, Kitty. And we now have a rather dear lease to contend with."

"It's an heirloom bracelet," Mellie explained. "Lady Dorsett will pay anything to get it back."

"Very well," I said. "I bow to your reasoning."

"Fifty pounds it is," Emma agreed.

"Thank you," Mellie exclaimed, all bright eyes. "I won't let you down." And off she went.

Just as Emma returned to her folders, a light knock sounded at the office door.

"Come in," I called.

Betsy stepped inside, her cheeks flushed with quiet excitement. Her red curls were pinned in their usual tidy twist, though a few stubborn ones had escaped to frame her face. She wore her brightest smile—the one that usually accompanied good news or a perfectly reconciled set of accounts.

"Sorry to interrupt," she said briskly. "I'd like to take the afternoon off, if that's not an inconvenience. Neville and I are planning to look at a few flats—for after the wedding, of course. We'd like something close to the Underground and not too far from our new office."

"How exciting!" I said. "Everything in order?"

"Perfectly," she replied with unmistakable pride. "The accounts are balanced and the ledgers are up to date. Triple-checked."

"Of course, you may take time to go flat hunting," Emma

said. "I'm only surprised you haven't reorganized the national budget."

Betsy grinned. "Tempting. But for now, I'll settle for a desk that isn't crammed into a broom cupboard."

"You'll have one," I promised. "With a door that closes and —if you're very lucky—a proper chair."

"I'm holding you to that." She gave us both a quick nod, then darted off with the efficiency of someone who'd already memorized the train schedule.

Emma shook her head fondly. "She needn't worry. She's already been assigned a proper office in the new place. Sunlight, shelving, a locking cabinet, and a door that doesn't creak."

"And a desk that doesn't double as the supply shelf?" I asked.

"With drawers," Emma added solemnly. "Several."

"Well then," I said, grinning, "she may never leave."

"Only to get married," Emma replied, returning to her notes. "And even then, I suspect she'll have the ledger balanced before she walks down the aisle."

As Betsy departed, I heard the click of a typewriter from down the corridor—rapid, rhythmic, and unmistakably efficient.

Doris Perkins, our newest hire, had already proven herself indispensable. Young, brisk, and blessed with boundless cheer, she brought the sort of energy that could make even the most reluctant client sit up straight. In only two weeks, she'd memorized our schedule, color-coded the appointment ledger, and begun answering the telephone in a tone so perky it could slice through fog. She was the sort of person who tidied things that weren't hers, labeled drawers no one had asked her to label, and somehow made us all feel slightly behind schedule.

The main telephone rang at the reception desk. A

moment later, Doris appeared in Emma's doorway, brisk as ever.

"Lady Emma," she announced, "Lord Marlowe is on the telephone. He says it isn't urgent."

Emma set down her pen with a composed nod. "Thank you, Doris. I'll take it here." She lifted her receiver with a smile. "Hello, darling. Hold a moment. I have Kitty in my office."

That was my cue to leave, if I ever heard one. Rising from my chair, I said, "I'd best get on with the Harwood case. If I'm not back by teatime, send biscuits. I'll be in desperate need by then."

"If you find the will," Emma replied smartly, "make a copy."

"And if I find a body?"

Her grin was quick. "Then Robert is your man."

Quite sensible. Robert was, after all, a Detective Chief Inspector at Scotland Yard. "Understood," I said, sweeping out the door—infidelity, forged paintings, and a kleptomaniac grand dame swirling in my wake.

CHAPTER 3

A VISIT TO AN ANTIQUITIES SHOP

*T*wo mornings after our supper party at Rutledge House, I paid a visit to *Rutland & Merton, Antiquaries*, the shop Robert had once discovered by chance while seeking shelter from a raging downpour. He had returned home soaked to the skin but full of enthusiasm, speaking in a way that betrayed genuine excitement. He described cabinets crowded with relics, manuscripts that seemed to whisper of forgotten hands, and a proprietor whose eye for provenance was matched only by his relish for secrets.

I had never stepped inside myself, though I had half-promised Robert I would one day. Now seemed the perfect opportunity.

There was something oddly charming about antiquities shops—the scent of time clinging to polished wood and worn leather, the hush of reverence that hangs over forgotten treasures. Rutland & Merton's was no exception.

Tucked discreetly between a gentlemen's haberdashery and a solicitor's office off Chancery Lane, its leaded-glass windows gave the impression of a place where secrets went to retire.

I paused a moment outside, studying my own reflection amid the dulled gleam of old coins and ivory chessmen displayed in the front window. The glass was faintly warped, making my image ripple like a ghost between centuries. A shiver ran through me—half from the brisk April wind, half from the peculiar gravity the place seemed to exude.

I pushed open the door, and a silver bell announced my entrance with a tone so delicate it might have belonged to a seventeenth-century drawing room. The air inside was warmer than the street, heavy with the mingled scents of beeswax, old paper, and a faint trace of pipe smoke clinging to the rafters.

Cabinets of curiosities stood like sentries, each one filled with relics from long ago—snuff boxes, carved cameos, gilded miniatures, and fragile pages encased in glass. Narrow aisles wound between them, and the hush was such that my own footsteps sounded impertinent. Dust motes swirled in the weak sunlight filtering through the leaded panes, transforming the air itself into something venerable.

A small sound drew my eye. I turned to find Mister Merton emerging from a side aisle. His spectacles perched halfway down his nose, giving him the air of a slightly distracted scholar, though I had already learned from Robert that nothing escaped him. He was tidily dressed, coat buttoned, collar starched, and a faintly amused expression in his eye as though everything and everyone existed to provide him some private entertainment.

"Lady Rutledge," came the cheerful greeting. "I was hoping you might pay me a visit."

I smiled, slipping off my gloves and tucking them neatly

into my handbag. "We were so pleased to have you at supper the other evening. I trust you enjoyed yourself?"

"Very much," he said with a small bow. "Your table was most gracious, and the company even more so. I count it a privilege to have been included."

"I am glad to hear it." I let my gaze travel slowly over the nearest cabinet, where a Roman oil lamp sat beside a medieval reliquary, incongruous yet somehow harmonious. "I've come not only to see for myself the wonders Robert has praised to the skies, but also in search of a gift. Something rare. Preferably ink-stained. Possibly a little dusty."

"For Lord Rutledge?" he guessed, eyes twinkling.

"Just so. He is difficult to surprise and harder still to impress. But rare books generally manage the trick."

"In that case," he said, beckoning, "follow me."

We wound our way through the narrow shelves, my skirt brushing against ancient wood, past cabinets filled with medieval seals and Tudor coins. I felt as though we were slipping backward through time itself. Eventually we reached a small alcove tucked behind a faded tapestry of Queen Elizabeth I. There, nestled like a secret, was a glass case holding half a dozen books.

"I acquired this one just last week," he said, carefully unlocking the case with a little flourish. "An early English translation of Lucretius—*On the Nature of Things*. Slight foxing at the margins, but the binding is original."

I leaned closer. The pages were uneven, as though cut by hand, the ink faded to a soft brown. Exactly the sort of thing Robert would find fascinating—science and poetry entwined in ancient vellum. For a moment I pictured his face lighting with delight as he unwrapped it, the lines of care that office and responsibilities etched upon him giving way to boyish eagerness.

"I'll take it," I said at once. "Robert will think me brilliant."

"You are brilliant, Lady Rutledge," Merton replied with a grin. He drew a length of fine paper toward him and began to wrap the volume with deliberate care, folding the corners crisply, as if the ceremony mattered nearly as much as the gift itself. Then, as his fingers tied the string with practiced ease, his glance flicked toward me.

"Am I wrong in assuming this visit isn't solely about a gift for Lord Rutledge?"

I tilted my head, feigning innocence. "Oh?" He had struck true, of course, but I wasn't about to give the whole game away.

His smile deepened. "At your supper, I mentioned something rather ... incendiary."

"You caught me out," I admitted with a soft laugh. "How clever of you. I confess, I haven't stopped thinking of it since. Curiosity has always been one of my besetting sins." I let the admission hang for a moment, then added more softly, "Won't you tell me more?"

He glanced about the alcove, as though the tapestry itself might carry tales to untrustworthy ears, and lowered his voice. "It's an account from the seventeenth century. Private, unsigned, but authenticated. It describes a series of meetings held just days before the Great Fire. A gathering of men—some of them high-ranking—discussing how best to manage a ... political inconvenience."

My brow rose. "What sort of inconvenience?"

"The Queen," he said, voice low. "Catherine of Braganza."

I drew in a sharp breath. Catherine. The name was more than history to me; it was memory. My governess had spoken of her during my lessons, weaving tales of the lonely Portuguese princess who had crossed the sea to marry a king, only to find herself mistrusted by his people. I could still recall sitting at the schoolroom window as a child, chin propped on my hand, listening wide-eyed while Miss Whitcombe described how Londoners had blamed their queen for plague and fire, how pamphleteers painted her as a foreign witch when she was guilty of nothing more than her faith and her birth.

Those stories had sparked my imagination, filling my mind with images of a brave young woman trapped in a court of vipers, her every glance misread, her every word twisted. I had felt for her then with a child's fervent sympathy, and now—hearing Merton's words—I felt it all over again.

To think that men of power had truly conspired against her, men who had bowed in her presence while plotting her downfall, sent a chill racing down my spine.

"It suggests that a plot was in motion," he went on, "something meant to remove her or damage her influence at court. It speaks of a scandal. A betrayal. And it includes a name." He paused, savoring the moment. "An ancestor of someone quite powerful today. A Cabinet minister, in fact."

To imagine that such treachery might still cast its shadow across a family name in 1925 was almost too much to fathom. I folded my arms tightly across my chest, more to steady myself than from doubt. "You are certain?"

"I am. I have verified the name through records. If this becomes public knowledge and tied to treason, it could discredit the entire family line."

A gleam lit his eyes—not fear, but relish. He looked positively enlivened by the thought, as though he had stumbled upon a delightful puzzle rather than a weapon capable of shattering lives.

"Mr. Merton, forgive me for saying so," I said slowly, "but you sound almost gleeful at the prospect of someone's ruin."

He chuckled softly, utterly untroubled. "History is rarely polite, Lady Rutledge. It favors those who seize it. A well-timed revelation can ruin dynasties or elevate commoners. It has always been so."

A cold unease tightened in my chest. He meant to wield this discovery—not guard it. Did he not see that secrets of such magnitude would not remain tidy within his shop, wrapped up like one of his rare books? That powerful men would go to any lengths—any lengths—to silence him?

"What do you intend to do with it?" I asked, my voice sharper than I intended.

He gave a slow, pleased smile, the smile of a man who believes himself the master of a dangerous game. "Hold a private auction. A gathering of collectors. Let the highest bidder decide what becomes of it."

My pulse flickered uneasily. He meant to profit from it. And in doing so, he would become the agent of another man's destruction, heedless of the danger to himself. "You cannot be serious."

"Entirely."

"This is dangerous, Merton. You have stumbled across something much larger than provenance and paper. If this falls into the wrong hands—"

"It fell into mine," he said calmly. "And I intend to be very careful with it."

"Lock. It. Up." I leaned forward, lowering my voice to match his. "I mean it. Whatever this is, it does not want to stay buried. And someone—possibly more than one someone—may go to great lengths to keep it hidden. They will not stop at ruining reputations. They will come for you."

He gave a small, indulgent nod, as though humoring a nervous child. "I appreciate your concern. But I know exactly what I am doing."

I was not so sure. I had seen what people were willing to

do for far less than a manuscript that could topple a minister. As I stepped back into the street a few minutes later, the spring wind tugging at my coat and the city's noise rising around me, I could not rid myself of the conviction that Mr. Merton had just placed himself in terrible peril. And he would pay for his hubris with his life.

CHAPTER 4

A TRAGIC DEATH

*S*aturday mornings at our Eaton Square home had become my favorite ritual. No pressing engagements. No society obligations. Just strong coffee, a warm fire, and the comfort of Robert quietly working his way through a plate of eggs while I lingered over toast with marmalade and pretended not to eye his last strip of bacon.

The breakfast room overlooked our small back garden—clipped hedges, neat gravel paths, and the stubborn roses that refused to surrender to London soot. Sunlight streamed through the windows, striking the silver toast rack and glinting off Robert's teacup, while the fire in the grate provided a cheerful counterpoint to the late spring chill.

Robert was buried in the *Times Literary Supplement*, his expression as serious as though the balance of English letters depended upon his attention. I had my coffee, eggs just the way I liked them, and the noble intention of not stealing from his plate.

"Don't think I don't notice," Robert said dryly from behind the periodical, just as my fork hovered near his bacon.

"I've no idea what you mean," I replied, sipping my coffee with studied innocence. "It's hardly theft if you weren't eating it."

"One might argue possession is nine-tenths of the law," he murmured, spearing another bite of egg with maddening calm.

"Ah, but the remaining tenth belongs to cunning." I snatched the bacon with a grin before he could react.

He gave me a look that was equal parts mock sternness and indulgence. "You're incorrigible."

"And you're predictable," I said sweetly, savoring my prize.

He folded the *Supplement* and set it aside, his expression shifting from amusement to intent. "I meant to ask you about your visit to Merton's shop. I should have asked last night, but it was past two when I finally came in."

"I waited for you as long as I could, darling. But I'm afraid I fell asleep." I tilted my head at him. "What kept you so late?"

"A gang we've been watching decided to make their move," he said, reaching for his tea. "Arms trafficking. We caught them in the act and spent half the night dragging them back to the Yard for questioning."

"That explains the circles under your eyes," I said softly, covering his hand with mine. "You must be exhausted."

"Not enough to forget about you." He raised my hand to his lips and kissed it. "Now, tell me about what you discovered at Merton's."

"The manuscript allegedly points toward treason of an ancestor of a current Cabinet minister. He said it had been authenticated. If true, it could ruin a man's life. I pointed out the obvious, that he was putting his life in danger. But he brushed my warning aside with a confidence I found almost insulting. He seemed to believe himself untouchable."

Robert's mouth tightened. "Arrogance makes a man careless."

"Exactly. I left the shop more uneasy than when I entered. He was so certain nothing could touch him. I think he will do the opposite of what I advised."

Robert leaned back in his chair, thoughtful. "If trouble comes, he'll have walked straight into it."

Before I could answer, the door opened and the footman entered with the morning paper, neatly folded. Robert set aside his teacup and reached for it, slipping the *Supplement* to one side.

He spread the paper across his plate, scanning the front page with the intent focus that always made me feel as though nothing else in the world existed. His eyes narrowed. The corner of the page crackled beneath his fingers.

"What is it?" I asked, leaning forward.

He didn't answer at once, only drew a long breath through his nose. Then he folded the paper toward me and tapped a column with one finger.

ANTIQUITIES DEALER MURDERED

I stared at the headline, my coffee cooling in its cup. *Merton.*

Shortly after sunrise, the body of a well-dressed gentleman was discovered on the southern end of London Bridge by a deliveryman en route to a warehouse. The deceased has been identified as Mr. Oswald Merton, proprietor of Rutland & Merton, Antiquaries, a respected shop specializing in rare manuscripts and historical objects. Scotland Yard has not yet released a cause of death, though sources suggest foul play is suspected. A witness reported hearing an argument in the early hours, but no suspect has been identified.

I set down my cup with care, as though the porcelain itself might shatter beneath my fingers. The arrogant tilt of

Merton's chin, the dismissive wave of his hand when I'd warned him — all of it flashed before me in an instant. I pressed my lips together. "He didn't take my advice. And now—"

"Now it's a murder case," he said, his voice low and grim.

"London Bridge," I whispered. "I warned him, Robert. He laughed at me."

Robert's jaw tightened. "And he paid for it with his life."

"It feels like my failure," I said, the words escaping before I could stop them. "If I'd pressed harder, if I'd—"

"You'd have changed nothing," Robert interrupted gently but firmly. "A man like Merton doesn't bend until he's broken. Unfortunately, that's exactly what's happened."

He scanned the rest of the article, his eyes narrowing. "If he was found on the bridge, it wasn't a random assault. Whoever killed him knew he'd be there."

The fire popped in the grate, a sharp crack that made me jump. Robert folded the paper and fixed me with the steady gaze I knew too well. It was the look that meant I was about to be treated less as a wife and more as a witness.

"Tell me everything about your visit. Who was in the shop when you arrived?"

"Only Merton. No clerk, no assistant."

Robert's mouth thinned. "What did he say about the manuscript?"

I drew in a breath, recalling the alcove at the shop, the way Merton had cast a furtive glance toward the tapestry before lowering his voice. "He claimed it was an account from the seventeenth century — private, unsigned, but authenticated. It describes a series of meetings held just days before the Great Fire of London. Gatherings of powerful men, some of them high-ranking, discussing how best to manage what he called a 'political inconvenience.'"

Robert's brow arched. "And what was that?"

"The Queen," I said quietly. "Catherine of Braganza."

He set his cup down with a soft click, his expression sharpening.

"At first I thought it an exaggeration," I went on, "but he spoke with such relish. He said the account suggests there was a plot — something meant to damage her influence at court, perhaps even to remove her. And he insisted the document includes a name. An ancestor of someone still in power today. A Cabinet minister."

Robert let out a low breath through his nose. "If true, it would be dynamite."

"I know." I clasped my arms tightly, steadying myself as old memories stirred. "My governess used to tell me stories of Catherine — the Portuguese princess who crossed the sea to wed a king, only to be mistrusted by his people. Londoners blamed her for plague and fire, branded her a witch because of her birth and her faith. I pitied her then with all the fervor of a child. When I heard Merton speak, I pitied her again. To imagine that such treachery truly took place — and that the shadow of it might still ruin a family name two centuries later—"

I broke off, shaking my head. "It chills me, Robert. And yet he spoke of it as though it were a prize to be flaunted, not a danger to be guarded."

Robert's jaw tightened. "Boasting in public, while holding evidence that could topple a man in government. He was a fool."

"A proud, arrogant fool," I agreed softly.

Robert's mouth thinned. "Did you notice anyone following you when you left the shop? Anyone lingering nearby?"

I shook my head. "No one. Just the usual hustle and bustle of city traffic. I felt eyes on me, perhaps, but it may only have been my imagination."

He tapped the folded paper against his palm. "Then you may very well be one of the last people to see him alive."

The words hung in the sunlit room like smoke.

I drew a careful breath. "If the Yard is to have any hope of finding his killer, they should be told about the manuscript."

Robert's gaze met mine, steady and intent. "And they will be. But not because of what he told you in private. I will not have your name linked to his death in any way." His voice sharpened slightly, the protective note unmistakable. "He declared it at supper loudly enough for half the room to hear, and that is more than sufficient. I'll make it clear to the Yard that his own boasting drew attention to him."

He rose, folding the paper beneath his arm with quiet finality. For a moment he studied me, the weight of his gaze as penetrating as any question.

"The temptation must be great to involve yourself. You knew the victim and what he revealed. But I implore you, Catherine, leave this one be. Dangerous people have already killed Merton. Heaven only knows what they would do to you."

I managed a faint smile, tracing the rim of my coffee cup as though it were the most absorbing thing in the world. He knew me too well to expect a promise, and I had no intention of giving one.

His sigh carried equal parts resignation and affection. "So be it." He leaned down, pressed a soft kiss to my lips, and whispered against my cheek, "At least promise me you'll be careful."

"Of course, darling."

He shook his head with a soft smile, then left me — bound for the Yard and the wheels of officialdom.

Of course, I had no intention of sitting idle. Merton's smirk still lingered in my memory. He'd been a proud, arrogant fool. But he hadn't deserved to be murdered for his arrogance.

I stared into the dying fire, weighing what Robert had said. Scotland Yard would treat it as a case, file it into their ledgers, and chase the obvious leads. But I had been in that shop. I had heard Merton's voice and seen the gleam of self-satisfaction in his eyes. I knew the kind of enemies such arrogance could breed.

If the manuscript truly existed—and I believed it did—then Merton's murder was about far more than theft or revenge. It was about secrets powerful enough to kill for.

I could not sit still, not when I already held threads the Yard would overlook. But to pull at them, I would need a reason, a door through which to step into the investigation. And that meant speaking to Merton's widow. She would want answers, and I—as the last to warn her husband—might be in the best position to give them.

CHAPTER 5

A WIDOW'S PLEA

*B*y late morning I had retreated to my parlor, the breakfast room seeming far too bright for brooding. The fire here was quieter, the shadows deeper, a place I could think. My coffee sat forgotten on the side table while I stared into the grate and tried to order my thoughts.

It would be crass—unforgivable, even—to appear uninvited on Mrs. Merton's doorstep in the wake of her husband's death. And yet if anyone might grant me a reason to involve myself, it would be his widow. She would want answers, and I might be the one to help her find them. Still, there was no polite way to intrude upon her grief.

The sudden trill of the telephone broke the stillness. I rose quickly to answer it. The line in the parlor was a small indulgence of mine. Its summons always felt oddly direct, as though the caller had stepped unannounced into my private sitting room.

"Lady Rutledge?" The voice on the other end was soft but strained, as though every syllable cost her dearly.

"Yes."

"This is Margaret Merton." A ragged breath carried down the line. "I beg your pardon for troubling you ... but I scarcely know where to turn. I am calling because ... because Oswald—"

"I know, Mrs. Merton," I said quickly, my voice softening. "I was heartsick to read of it in the morning paper. Please accept my deepest condolences. Your husband's death is a dreadful tragedy."

For a moment only silence answered, and then she managed, her voice breaking, "It hardly seems real. Only yesterday he sat across from me at breakfast and now ..." Another breath shuddered down the line. "I cannot make sense of it. To lose him so suddenly, so cruelly—"

"You have all my sympathy," I murmured. "If there is anything I can do for you, anything at all, you need only ask."

"That is why I have called," she said at last, gathering herself with visible effort. "Might you ... might you visit me? There are things I must speak of, matters the police will not understand. I believe you may be the only one who can."

"My dear Mrs. Merton, of course I shall come," I assured her. "At once."

BY EARLY AFTERNOON I stood before the Merton residence, a sober brick townhouse on a quiet street not far from St. James's Square. Heavy curtains had already been drawn across the windows, shrouding the house in gloom, and a strip of black crepe hung on the polished brass knocker.

I was shown into a darkened drawing room, the mirrors veiled, the lamps turned low. The air smelled faintly of lavender water, no doubt pressed upon Mrs. Merton in hopes of steadying her nerves. Her pearl-gray mourning dress, though subdued, made her look even more ghostlike than her pale cheeks and wide eyes would allow.

"Mrs. Merton." I took her hand gently, pressing it with a firmness meant to reassure. "I am so very sorry. Your husband's death is a loss keenly felt."

Her lips trembled, and she gave a small shake of her head. "It hardly seems possible. Only yesterday he left this house full of life and plans. And now..." Her words faltered as she pressed a handkerchief to her lips.

I guided her back into her chair and sat close beside her. "You need not speak of it if it pains you too deeply," I said softly.

But she shook her head with fragile determination. "No. You must understand, Lady Rutledge. They said he was found... on London Bridge at sunrise." Her voice caught, and her eyes brimmed. "To imagine him lying there in the cold, without me ... without anyone—" She broke off again, her composure splintering.

I laid a hand lightly on her arm. "You are not alone in this, Mrs. Merton. If there is anything I may do—anything at all—you need only ask."

She lowered her handkerchief and looked at me then, her gaze raw but steady. "That is why I wanted to see you. My husband spoke of you after your visit. He said you pressed him on certain matters." Her breath wavered. "I believe you may know more than the police ever will."

Mrs. Merton dabbed at her eyes, then folded the handkerchief with painstaking care, as though neatness might steady her. "Oswald was not an easy man, Lady Rutledge. He was proud ... too proud at times. But he was my husband, and whatever his faults, he did not deserve to die like that."

"No, he did not," I agreed.

Her gaze flickered to the darkened window. "He had been restless of late. Even at our supper table, his mind seemed elsewhere. At first, I thought it was business. He was always buying, selling, bargaining. But last week he began speaking of a manuscript. He was—" She swallowed hard. "He was boastful. Too boastful. He said it would make his name. That no one could ignore him once it was known what he possessed."

My pulse quickened. "Did he tell you what was in it?"

She shook her head, the gesture seeming to drain her strength. "No. Only that it was dangerous knowledge. I told him not to speak of it in company, that it would only invite envy or worse. But he laughed at me." Her voice broke again, soft and bitter. "He laughed, Lady Rutledge. He paid me no heed. And now—"

"You did what any devoted wife would do," I said gently. "You tried to protect him. His death is not on you."

Her eyes filled afresh, but this time she held my gaze with quiet intensity. "The police will see only robbery, or some quarrel gone wrong. They will not understand how reckless his words could be, or how they might have placed him in danger. But you were there at his shop. You spoke to him. You may know what they cannot."

"Did he show you the manuscript?"

She drew a steadying breath. "He brought it home two nights ago, but no, he didn't show it to me. He took it back to the shop and locked it away in the safe. He said it was more secure there."

"Is it still there?" I asked.

Her voice broke. "A constable allowed me into the premises this morning. I checked the safe. The manuscript was gone."

"You think it was stolen?"

"Not as far as I could see," she whispered. "Nothing was

taken. Not the ivory figurines. Not the Georgian snuffboxes. But the manuscript was no longer in the safe. I'm sure someone killed him for it."

"Was the shop rifled through?"

"No. It was neat as a pin."

Seemingly, no one had broken into the shop. More than likely, Merton had taken the manuscript with him. Maybe to show someone? "Did he ever mention who might be interested? Potential buyers?"

"He was secretive," she admitted. "But I overheard him on the telephone two nights ago, arranging what sounded like a private showing."

"He mentioned an auction to me," I said.

"Yes, exactly. He spoke of two names—Sir Peregrine Loxley and Professor George Whitford—and then he mentioned someone at the Ministry. He didn't give the man's name, only that he wished to attend."

"That could be important," I murmured.

"I thought it odd," Mrs. Merton said, frowning faintly. "Why should a government man care about a seventeenth-century manuscript?"

"Because the contents could ruin someone," I said softly, more to myself than to her. "And now the document is gone."

"Yes," she whispered. "Taken from a secure safe."

Taking a deep breath, I gazed at her with as much kindness as I could summon. "As I see it, Mrs. Merton, someone wanted that document, and he was willing to kill for it." Merton could not be allowed to live. He'd seen the manuscript and knew what was in it.

Mrs. Merton squared her shoulders and set down her cup with a decisive clink. "That's what I believe as well. I want you to find out who did this. Scotland Yard will poke around, ask a few questions, then declare it a robbery gone wrong. But you and I both know that's not what this was."

Clearly, she was made of sterner stuff. "I agree."

"I'll pay whatever fee you require. Lord Rutledge as well, if needed."

I reached over and covered her hand with mine. "No fee will be required. I'm handling this matter pro bono." Mrs. Merton would be incurring enough expenses from her husband's death.

Her lip trembled. "Thank you."

"I need a list of everyone your husband spoke to this past week. Anyone who visited the shop. Any unusual deliveries or meetings."

"I will check with his clerk. But there was one man," she said slowly. "He came in two days ago—tall, well-dressed, with a walking stick and a thick foreign accent. He asked after rare items from the Stuart court. Oswald was… evasive."

"Did you catch his name?"

"No. But he left a card. I'll find it for you."

As she rose and moved toward what must be her late husband's desk, I stood and looked out the window. The street below bustled as usual—children chasing one another, a delivery cart rattling by, a pair of nuns making their way toward the bakery. The world didn't stop for grief. It never had.

Mrs. Merton returned and handed me a plain calling card with a single name embossed in black ink.

Monsieur Alphonse Duret

Collector – Paris

"He was also at the British Library lecture Oswald gave last month. Seemed harmless. Charming, even."

"I'll find him." I'd assign that task to Mellie. She had a rare gift for locating individuals, including those who didn't want to be found. And, having been raised in a French convent, she spoke fluent French.

As I slipped the card into my handbag, Mrs. Merton reached for my hand again. Her grip was firmer this time.

"Don't let them get away with it, Lady Rutledge."

"I won't."

Outside, the wind had picked up. A chill slid through the afternoon, making the rooftops shiver. Somewhere out there, someone had killed for a secret. I meant to find them ... before they decided one murder wasn't enough.

CHAPTER 6

NOTES BY THE FIRE

*T*he lamps were already lit by the time I returned to Eaton Square. The under-butler, a sober young man, opened the door in Mister Black's stead.

"Milady." He bowed, his manner stiff with effort, as though determined to prove himself worthy of the post while our butler recovered from his broken leg.

"Good evening, Pritchard. Has Lord Rutledge returned home?" I asked, slipping off my gloves.

"He's in the library, ma'am," he said, while relieving me of my coat. "He requested that supper be served as soon as you arrived. Does that meet with your approval?"

"Oh, yes, thank you." It had been several hours since my last meal, and my stomach was making its protest known.

I entered the library to find Robert seated before the fire with a glass of wine in hand, the flames playing across the strong planes of his face. As soon as he saw me, he rose at once, his expression warm and touched with that loving look I'd long appreciated.

"Been sleuthing, dear?" His tone was mild, but the glint in his eyes betrayed a quiet amusement.

I swiftly crossed the room and kissed his cheek. "You know me so well. But believe it or not, I was summoned." I sank into the wingback chair opposite him, smoothing my skirt across my knees. "Mrs. Merton telephoned this morning. She begged me to come."

A corner of his mouth lifted as he swirled the wine in his glass. "And of course you couldn't resist."

"Would you have?"

"No," he admitted, settling back into his chair. "If she'd requested my help, I would have called on her."

"Which is exactly what I did. And now you won't have to."

"Oh, I won't be investigating the matter." He reached for the claret decanter, refilled his own glass, then lifted the decanter toward me in silent question. "Would you like some?"

"Yes, thank you." It had turned rather chilly.

As he handed me the glass, he added, "The superintendent assigned another chief detective inspector to the case. Raphael Simpson. Newly promoted. Still wet behind the ears, but very eager."

"Do you think he'll give this investigation its due?" I asked lightly, though inwardly I was dead serious. Eager was one thing. Competent was another matter entirely.

Robert settled back into his chair. "I think he will be very diligent. But he lacks imagination."

I smiled. "Then it's just as well I've taken an interest in the matter." Imagination had always been my strongest weapon. It will aid the investigation if Simpson fails to detect the less obvious.

Leaning forward, he rested his elbows on his knees. "Shall we compare notes?"

"Absolutely."

Before either of us could say more, Pritchard appeared, directing two footmen with the supper trays. Our meal was arranged on the small dining table set near the fire, where two chairs had already been placed. The covers were lifted, releasing the aroma of roasted chicken and thyme, flanked by crisp potatoes and a dish of stewed apples.

Robert carved for us both, added the potatoes and apples, and set my plate before me with quiet precision. It was one of his small, unspoken habits. He liked to care for me. I pretended to mind. But truthfully, I found it comforting. By silent agreement, we satisfied our hunger before tackling the subject uppermost in our minds. The steady clink of silverware and the crackle of the fire were the only sounds in the room.

Once the supper plates were cleared and dessert and coffee were served, Robert leaned back. "Do you want to go first, or shall I?"

"Oh, you, by all means." I leaned forward, eager. "I'm anxious to hear what you've learned."

"The medical examiner was swift with his report." His tone was measured, betraying little, though the gravity in his eyes told me enough. "Oswald Merton was struck down by a single blow to the head. His body was found at the southern end of London Bridge. A deliveryman heard raised voices followed by a cry, but didn't see anything. The killer vanished into the fog before he found Merton, quite dead."

"Was anything stolen?" I asked.

"No." He ticked the items off with a faint gesture of his hand. "His watch, his rings, his purse—all untouched."

"Merton must have had the manuscript on him. They killed him for it."

"That's the most likely explanation." Robert's gaze sharpened, his expression tightening with the weight of certainty.

"He kept it tucked in his safe at the shop. But when Mrs. Merton checked it this morning, it was empty. And the safe had not been forced open."

He sat back, gaze thoughtful. "Merton must have arranged a meeting, although whether at London Bridge or somewhere else remains to be seen. Whoever killed him knew he was carrying it with him and ended his life so he could take the manuscript."

"That makes sense. But I also think he was killed because he knew what was in it." I toyed with my wineglass, turning it slowly. "He'd read the manuscript. He knew the names contained within it and had connected them to someone high up in the government. Someone whose life would be ruined if the contents of that manuscript were ever made public." I gazed at Robert. "But what could they have said that Merton would risk bringing the manuscript with him?"

"Merton seemed to be motivated by money. Chances are, they offered him a great deal of it to take a simple peek."

"That tracks with what Mrs. Merton said."

While Robert took several moments to think things through, I enjoyed a bite of the creme brûlée and sipped my coffee. "But London Bridge seems an odd place to choose for an examination."

"More than likely, that was not the meeting place. Somewhere close to it, though, so his killer knew he would travel through there."

"By foot and at sunrise? It would be rather chilly at that time of day."

"Great questions for which we'll need answers."

"The killer picked the right time, though." I leaned back, picturing it. "At that hour, they would not have been easily seen. What with all the early morning fog. And even if someone had, a description would be next to useless." I hesitated. "There were no other witnesses other than the deliveryman?"

"No. But the Yard is putting the word out. Something should appear in the papers tomorrow. Maybe someone will come forward." Robert tipped his glass toward me. "So what did you learn from Mrs. Merton?"

I set aside my spoon and folded my napkin with deliberate care. "She is grief-stricken, of course. Pale as a ghost, but determined to find her husband's killer. She said Merton had been restless, distracted, and that he had taken the manuscript home briefly before locking it in the safe at the shop. As I mentioned, it wasn't there this morning."

Robert's jaw tightened, though he said nothing.

"She also overheard him on the telephone," I continued. "Arranging a private showing. Three interested parties—Sir Peregrine Loxley, Professor George Whitford, and someone at the Ministry. Merton did not share that name with her. Only told her he intended to attend."

Robert leaned back, steepling his fingers. "Without a name, it'll be hard to track him down. Did she mention anything else about the Ministry man?"

"Only that her husband seemed eager for his interest." I reached for my reticule and drew out the card. "Someone else showed interest as well. Monsieur Alphonse Duret. A French collector. She said he visited the shop two days ago, asking questions about Stuart artifacts. Left this behind."

Robert turned the card over thoughtfully, his thumb grazing the embossed letters. "I know the name. I've seen him at an auction or two. Smooth as cream. But a man who asks after Stuart relics just as a manuscript naming seventeenth-century plotters disappears?" His eyes lifted to mine. "That stinks of calculation."

For a moment we both sat in silence, the firelight flickering over the rows of the library books. The clink of the clock on the mantel seemed suddenly very loud.

I leaned forward, elbows on the table. "So. We have Loxley, Whitford, a nameless Ministry man, and this Monsieur Duret. Which one do we pursue first?"

Robert raised an amused brow. "Is that the royal we? As in your friends and family, including me?"

I couldn't help smiling. "No friends and family. Only you. Ned and Lily are getting married in two months. We're moving offices to a new address, which means Emma must stay on top of that. Mellie is clamoring for more responsibility at the agency, although I think she could be helpful with Monsieur Duret. And Richard will soon be off for Oxford to lecture. I'm afraid that only leaves you and me. I won't be able to do this without you." I gazed at him somewhat sheepishly. "You don't mind, do you?"

"Of course not." He covered my hand with his own. "But those friends and family may have something to say. Knowing them, they'll want to keep a hand in. Ned's assistance would be especially useful. He's kept in touch with his friends at the Ministry of War. Somebody there is bound to know something."

"But would they be able to share? Official Secrets Act and all that."

"Yes, that is a problem."

I tapped the rim of my glass thoughtfully. "Why don't you start with Duret, since you've seen him at the occasional auction. I'm sure you can come up with a reason to talk to him."

"Won't be hard."

"I'll start with Loxley."

"Ask Marlowe about him. He might know him from his club."

I arched a brow, unconvinced. "Long shot, surely."

"You never know." He set down his glass with a quiet clink. "And talk to Richard about Professor Whitford. If he taught antiquities, Richard is bound to know of him."

I hid a smile behind my cup. "You are determined to draw others into our investigation."

He grinned at me. "I know how much you enjoy bossing us around."

I gave him a look of mock severity. "You are a devious, cunning man, Inspector."

He laughed and leaned across to pluck my spoon. "I aim to please." And then, in the next instant, he stole the last bite of my crème brûlée.

The beast.

CHAPTER 7

A WARNING OF DANGER

As it turned out, Marlowe was not familiar with Loxley, but Richard did indeed know Professor Whitford, a highly respected former Oxford professor with a wealth of knowledge about medieval manuscripts. My brother not only shared his telephone number and address but provided an introduction to Professor Whitford who agreed to see me that same day.

I wasn't quite sure what I'd expected of his residence—perhaps stacks of old newspapers, the scent of forgotten ink, or a looming suit of armor from an archaeological misadventure—but the house on Bedford Square was, in fact, rather ordinary. Respectable. Impeccably maintained, with not a speck of dust or disorder in sight.

As soon as I gave my name to the butler who opened the door, he offered a polite but perfunctory bow. Just enough courtesy for a gentlewoman, but not a whisper more. Understandable. I'd made the appointment under my maiden name and not my title.

"Miss Worthington," he said, stepping aside. "The professor is expecting you. If you would follow me?"

I was led down a paneled hallway where the electric lights were lit low against the afternoon gloom and shown into a drawing room lined with bookcases. The air was warm and dry, scented faintly with old vellum and something faintly medicinal. A tea service waited on the sideboard, untouched.

Professor Whitford rose from his chair as I entered. He was a tall man with a thatch of snow-white hair and—if Richard's description was to be trusted—a mind as sharp as a scalpel. While his dark suit bore an ink stain near the cuff, his spectacles glinted as if he'd just polished them.

"Miss Worthington. A pleasure to meet you."

"Thank you for receiving me on such short notice, Professor Whitford."

"Not at all. I rather expected someone might call."

That gave me pause. "About Mister Merton? Or about the manuscript?" We had already discussed the purpose of my visit, but not my specific reason for seeing *him*.

"Both. But let's do it over a cup of tea. Won't you take a seat?" He gestured toward the armchair opposite his own, then poured tea with a steadiness that belied his age. "I find tea helps lubricate a discussion. Don't you agree?"

"I do." I accepted the cup with a polite smile, though I had no intention of drinking just yet.

It was clear he didn't mean to leap directly into the heart of things. He was one of those gentlemen who believed in conversational foreplay—mild observations, a little weather talk, and perhaps a remark on the state of scholarship before any real business was broached.

I let my gaze wander as he settled back into his chair. The drawing room was lined floor to ceiling with well-tended bookcases, their shelves packed tight with spines cracked, probably by use and not neglect. A small globe stood near the fireplace, beside a faded armchair that bore the faint impress of many thoughtful hours. The only real ornamentation was a brass astrolabe perched on the mantel, its curves catching the low gleam of the electric sconces. A man of intellect, clearly. And discipline.

It was the sort of room one might expect to smell faintly of pipe smoke and chalk dust. Instead, it carried only the warm, clean scent of polished wood and faintly medicinal tea.

We sat for a moment in companionable quiet, the clink of porcelain the only sound between us. Professor Whitford added a lump of sugar to his cup with precise fingers, then stirred once, clockwise. I took a tentative sip of my own, the liquid pleasantly hot but faintly bitter. Certainly stronger than I preferred, though I didn't complain.

He sipped as well, eyes fixed on the steam curling above his cup, as though gathering his thoughts with the methodical patience of a man accustomed to long silences.

I waited. He'd earned the right to lead.

But when several quiet moments passed, I asked gently, "You knew Mr. Merton professionally, I assume?"

"I did." A faint smile softened the corners of his mouth. "We met some ten years ago at a symposium on Anglo-Dutch trade relics. He was clever, insatiably curious, and more of a scholar than many gave him credit for. We disagreed on almost everything, of course, but respectfully. That's a rarer gift than people think."

I nodded, keeping my tone neutral. "His widow mentioned your name. She said he'd recently consulted you." That's not what she said. But it made sense given his area of expertise.

Whitford gave a small grunt of acknowledgment. "He

paid me a visit about three weeks ago. Said he'd come into possession of a rather sensitive manuscript and wanted my thoughts on its authenticity."

"A manuscript from the seventeenth century?"

His gaze sharpened. "So you do know something about it."

"Only that it may have been tied to a plot against Queen Catherine of Braganza," I said carefully. "And that it may have named names."

"That is more than something, Miss Worthington." Whitford leaned back slightly, fingers drumming once against his teacup. "It was no forgery, I can tell you that."

Rather than ask about how he'd determined it was authentic, I took another tack. "What did the manuscript look like?"

Whitford's brow furrowed in thought. "Small. Bound in dark leather, quite worn. I couldn't say how many pages it held, but it had weight to it. He only allowed me to read a few lines, and even then, he handled it carefully. He never let it out of his sight."

"Was it damaged?"

"A bit. Some charring at the edges. I suspect it survived a fire at some point, though he never said as much. The pages I saw were coarse and yellowed, written in iron gall ink. Some sections were in cipher, others in a distinctly seventeenth-century hand. A diary, perhaps. Or a personal ledger. But intimate in tone. Confessional, you might say."

He paused, then added, "The portion he showed me—just a page and a half—was badly scorched at the edges but still legible. It referenced a group of men meeting in secret. Parliamentarians. Courtiers. A planned discrediting—or something even darker."

"Targeting the Queen?"

He nodded.

"Why her?"

He gave a wry smile. "Catherine was Portuguese, Catholic, and politically inconvenient. There were men who believed the crown would be stronger without a foreign bride to an English king. Men with ambition will use any excuse to carve out their own path to power."

"And the names?"

Whitford shook his head. "There were no names in the fragments I examined, only initials, and veiled language, references to rank, positions held at court. But Merton hinted that one of the names, perhaps in a later section, belonged to someone whose family still sits in the House of Lords."

I felt the faintest prick of unease. "So the danger lies not only in what it says, but in who it implicates."

"Exactly." He studied me. "I warned him to keep it hidden. To lock it away and tell no one else."

"Unfortunately, he didn't. Instead, he arranged for a private auction." I paused, watching him carefully. I suspected he'd been asked to attend, but I wanted to hear him say it. "Were you invited?"

"I was. It was to be held next week." He gave a rueful laugh. "I am an expert on antiquities, Miss Worthington. My pockets, unfortunately, would not have allowed me to bid. But I wanted to see more of the manuscript."

"You advised him against it, though."

"I did. But he paid me no heed." Whitford gave a rueful shake of his head. "He saw it as an opportunity. A way to finally claim his place among serious collectors and to sell it to the highest bidder."

He settled back into his seat, steepling his fingers. "Did you know Merton personally?"

"We met at supper just days ago. He was a guest in my

home. That's one of the reasons Mrs. Merton reached out to me."

"The other being, she knew of your reputation as a detective."

"Yes."

"Your husband, Lord Rutledge, is also a chief detective inspector at Scotland Yard, I believe."

"He is."

"I imagine he has something to say in the matter."

"He does, but it's quite confidential. I hope you understand." I tilted my head slightly, offering a polite smile.

I recognized the shift. He was asking the questions now—testing me, in his own way. I couldn't begrudge him a little probing, not after everything I'd asked of him. A fair exchange, to a point. But there were limits.

"Are you investigating the murder or the theft of the manuscript, Miss Worthington?"

"Both. You cannot separate the two."

He rose and crossed to the sideboard, pouring himself another cup of tea. "Merton treated it as a curio. An artifact to be sold to the highest bidder. But it was never simply that. It's a powder keg."

Taking his seat again, he said, "I will give you the same advice I gave to Merton. You must tread very carefully. Whoever now possesses that document may not even know its full contents. But those who do know? They will go to great lengths to keep it silent. Be careful who you talk to. What you say."

Outside, a distant clock began to chime the hour. It was time to go. But not before I asked him one last question.

"If I happen upon it—or fragments of it—will you examine them?"

"Yes," he said at once. "But bring them to me directly. And speak of it to no one."

As I stepped out into the grey London afternoon, a light rain had begun to fall. I wrapped my coat more tightly around me.

If what Whitford said was true—if there truly had been a plot against Queen Catherine, recorded in ink and protected for centuries—then someone had already killed to keep that secret buried.

And they wouldn't hesitate to kill again.

CHAPTER 8

THE FALL

The grey afternoon had deepened into a silvered haze of evening by the time I returned to Eaton Square. A light mist clung to the stones, turning the lamps to halos and painting the pavement in slick reflections. Pritchard opened the door at once, his posture straight despite the hour.

"Good evening, milady. Two notes have arrived for you, ma'am," he said, relieving me of my coat. "One from Lord Rutledge. The other arrived half an hour ago—marked urgent."

I carried both into the library, where a fire burned cheerfully. Robert's note was brief, neat, and apologetic. A case had taken an unexpected turn, so he would be staying late at Scotland Yard. He would not return in time for supper.

Bother! That was an unfortunate turn of events. I'd hoped to discuss my conversation with Professor Whitford with him. Robert always had a way of shedding light on such matters. Well, it would have to wait.

The second note bore Marlowe's crisp, masculine hand. He had found Loxley. The gentleman had agreed to speak with me and had provided a telephone number. But tonight was the only time he could receive me, as he was leaving town early the next morning.

I rang him at once.

After a servant answered with 'Loxley Residence,' another voice came on the line—smooth, low, and cultured in the way some men carry like a monocle.

"Miss Worthington," Loxley said. "I'm so pleased to hear from you. I understand you're investigating our mutual friend's untimely end?"

"I am. I was hoping we might speak, just briefly."

"Of course. I'll be at home all evening. Please come whenever it suits you." He ended the call with a courteous farewell.

As much as I longed to consult Robert, there was no time. Loxley was leaving tomorrow morning, and I could not risk missing him.

I took a quick bath, dressed in a dark business suit, and chose a hat and gloves, both stylish and restrained. By the time I descended to the foyer, Pritchard had already hailed a cab.

"Would you like a footman to accompany you, Lady Rutledge?"

I smiled. "No need. It's only a short call. I shan't be long."

After slipping into my evening coat, I let him open the door. The cool night closed round my shoulders like a whisper.

WISHING for a stretch of my legs before I arrived at the Loxley residence, I asked the cab to let me out near St. James's, not directly at the address Loxley had given me. I regretted the decision almost at once. The air had grown damp, and the fog was creeping low and steady. I felt certain my coiffured bob would soon fall to ruin. Quickening my pace, I passed a handful of pedestrians, each striding with brisk purpose, collars turned high. Seemingly, they were of a like mind.

Under the dim glow of a streetlamp, I checked the address once more, then moved forward until I spotted the house. It stood slightly back from the road, a narrow hedge guarding its wrought-iron gate. Warm light glowed from the upper windows, a welcome sight against the gathering fog. Still, something about the shadows clinging to the hedge made me quicken my steps.

Almost as soon as I dropped the knocker, the door opened. A liveried young man stood before me—not old enough to be a butler. A footman, most likely.

He ushered me into a stylishly appointed drawing room, where Sir Peregrine Loxley awaited me.

He rose to greet me, a slender figure dressed with the easy extravagance of a man who never left his tailor in peace. His evening coat was cut to perfection, his cravat secured with a jeweled pin that caught the lamplight, and his hair—gleaming chestnut—was brushed to a faultless sheen. A silver-topped walking stick rested against his chair, though I doubted he needed it.

His bow was courtly, his smile even more so, but there was a sharpness in his gaze that belied the languid elegance of his manner. This was a man accustomed to getting what he wanted, whether by charm, coin, or sheer persistence.

"Sir Peregrine," I said, inclining my head, "thank you for receiving me on such short notice."

He gave a graceful wave of his hand, as though brushing aside the notion of inconvenience. "My dear Lady Rutledge, for a lady of discernment and energy, my door is always open. Besides"—his eyes glinted with a keen intelligence—"when the subject is Merton and his manuscript, I should think the whole of London might knock, and I would still make time."

With a flick of his wrist, he indicated a tray on the sideboard. "May I offer you refreshment? Tea, perhaps? Or something stronger, should you prefer it?"

"Thank you, but nothing for me," I replied.

"In that case, with your permission—" He crossed to the sideboard and poured himself a measure of amber liquid, the crystal glass catching the firelight. "A touch of whiskey for fortification," he said, lifting it briefly in a gesture of apology before taking a slow, deliberate sip.

His gaze lingered on me over the rim of the glass. "You said you wished to discuss Merton—and the Stuart manuscript?" He set the glass down with deliberate care, the faintest smile touching his lips. "A rare volume indeed, and one I had very much hoped would come into my possession."

"Yes," I replied. "The manuscript seems to have stirred a great deal of interest. You had the opportunity to see it yourself?"

His eyes brightened. "Only a few pages, alas. Merton was fiercely protective. He scarcely allowed it from his sight. But what I saw was extraordinary. Seventeenth-century vellum, the hand precise, the ink hardly faded. Notes in the margin suggested more than mere record-keeping. I would have paid whatever price he asked."

"What sort of notes?" I asked quickly.

He regarded me with a touch of superiority, clearly savoring the moment. "Annotations, my dear lady. Curious references to allegiances and oaths. Hints of secret rendezvous. Enough to whet any collector's appetite. And more than enough to make certain men nervous."

"What men?" I pressed.

Loxley's smile deepened, though his eyes sharpened. "Ah, now that is the question, isn't it? Merton would never say. But I had the impression he enjoyed knowing others coveted what he held. It gave him a certain power."

I studied him in silence, weighing his words. It was clear he would go no further where the manuscript was concerned, not without some advantage to be gained. Very well. Best to turn the conversation another way.

"And Merton himself?" I asked. "How well did you know him?"

Loxley swirled the whiskey in his glass before answering. "Well enough to admire his eye for rarity. He understood the value of what he had, I'll grant him that. But Merton was no true scholar. To him, the manuscript was coin in the pocket —nothing more. He was perfectly willing to part with it to the highest bidder."

His mouth twisted faintly. "In the meantime, he relished the power it gave him. I believe he dangled it before someone who could not afford exposure and enjoyed watching them squirm. A dangerous game. In the end …" Loxley's shoulders lifted in a delicate shrug "… that game killed him."

"You make it sound as though you have some idea who Merton was toying with," I said, leaning forward. "Do you?"

For a moment Loxley's gaze met mine, steady and unblinking. Then he gave a short, dismissive laugh and raised his glass. "Speculation, Lady Rutledge, is a collector's vice. One I indulge only when it profits me."

The words were smooth, but the flicker in his eyes betrayed more than he wished to admit. He knew something —or someone—but the memory of Merton's fate had sealed his lips.

With no more knowledge to be obtained, I rose to my feet. "Thank you for your time, Sir Peregrine."

He bowed while still wearing that superior smile. "The pleasure was mine, dear lady."

"If you think of anything else, I would appreciate it if you would contact me," I said, smoothing my gloves.

"Of course," he said at once. "You have my word."

But as I met his gaze, I could not shake the sense that his promise was no more than courtesy. He would not dare say more—not when he feared he might be the next to fall.

As I was shown out, the footman didn't offer his assistance. Nor did he volunteer to hail a cab for me. Odd, to say the least.

I reasoned there might be a cab stand on the far side of St. James's Square, so I headed off in that direction. The fog hung low and even thicker than before, blurring the lamps into smudges of gold, dulling the usual noises to be found on the square. My footsteps echoed in the emptiness.

But at the corner of the square came a sound that set my nerves on edge—a footfall that did not belong to me.

A sharp turn of my head revealed only emptiness, the street behind swallowed in fog. As silence pressed close, a whisper of movement, no more than a shadow, skimmed the edge of my vision. But it was gone as soon as I sought it.

Wary, I quickened my pace.

The fog thickened, curling damp fingers through the lamplight until the square blurred into shapes half-formed. My breath rasped loud in my ears. I slipped a hand into my coat pocket, fingertips brushing the cool hilt of my little penknife—my one defense.

But then, a sharp crack of pain exploded at the back of my skull. The world spun sideways, my knees gave way, the pavement rushed up to meet me.

And darkness swallowed me whole.

CHAPTER 9

LONDON, 1666

AWAKENING IN ANOTHER TIME

A hand gripped my shoulder, shaking me from darkness.

"Up, my lady. Pray, stir yourself! The queen asks for you."

The Queen? *Queen Mary*? What could she want with me?

My eyes fluttered open to a chamber I did not recognize. Heavy damask hangings framed the bed, walls draped with rich tapestries, an air that smelled of beeswax and woodsmoke. A tall oak chair stood near the hearth, its carved arms gleaming in the candlelight. Nothing was familiar.

Could I be at Buckingham Palace? Why? How? The last thing I remembered was walking across St. James's Park. I had felt—more than seen—someone shadowing me. And then ... a blow. Pain. Darkness.

Obviously, I had been carried to this ... place. Whatever it was. But what was it?

A maidservant bent over me, curtsying anxiously. She was plain, capable-looking, of middling height. Her dark hair was tucked neatly beneath a white linen cap. Her gown was serviceable brown wool, the apron clean though patched at the hem, her sleeves rolled above steady, work-worn hands. Nothing in her appearance was remarkable save her eyes—clear, grey, watchful, and quick to measure.

"The queen requires your presence, my lady." Her tone held urgency.

Obviously, she wanted me to rise. But who spoke like that in this day and age? "The queen?" I managed, my voice rough.

"Her Majesty waits in her withdrawing chamber," the girl whispered. "She grows impatient, my lady. You must make haste."

As I pushed myself upright, the world spun. Swallowing hard, I willed myself to remain seated while I studied my surroundings. I was wearing a silk bedgown—quilted and trimmed with lace, finer than anything I had ever owned. Beside the bed, draped over a carved chair, lay a gown of crimson satin, its slashed sleeves and jeweled bodice unmistakably of an earlier age.

Surely I was dreaming. Or perhaps I was attending a masquerade? That would explain the gown. But I didn't recall an invitation to such a thing. The blow to my head could have scrambled my memory, though. Could this be a charade staged for my benefit? I gazed at the door on the far side of the bedchamber, half-expecting Robert to stroll through it dressed as a courtier from centuries past. Yes, that had to be it. I wished I could remember.

The maid leaned closer, lowering her voice. "You are pale, my lady. Shall I tell them you are indisposed?"

"No," I said quickly, my mind racing. Whatever this was, I needed to find out. "That will not be necessary."

I steadied myself against the bedpost, studying her more closely. "Who are you?"

The maid dropped another curtsy. "Anne, my lady. I have been set to your service since your former maid is no longer with us."

"No longer with us?" That could mean anything.

"She departed last month, my lady—married a cooper's son and returned to her kin in Southwark," Anne said briskly.

I swallowed hard. Well, at least that was a logical explanation. But the *queen* part was not. "Anne ... forgive me, but which queen is it who asks for me?"

Anne blinked in surprise. "Why, Her Majesty Queen Catherine, of course—Catherine of Braganza. She waits in her withdrawing chamber even now."

The name struck me like a blow. Catherine of Braganza—the Portuguese queen, Charles II's consort. That meant ... London, the plague years, the Restoration court. If this was a charade, it was quite an elaborate one

My heart seized on a single thought: Robert. Surely my husband would be here, ready to laugh with me over this strange pageant. "And Robert?" I asked quickly, almost tripping over the words. "My husband. Where is he?"

Anne's expression softened into sorrow. She lowered her gaze. "Ah, my lady... Captain Robert Halloran is not with us. God rest him. He was taken by the flux last winter." She hesitated, then added more gently, "The king himself spoke well of his service. You bear his memory in high honor."

The world tilted beneath me. Robert dead? The words rang false, yet Anne's eyes held no jest. My breath caught, and I clutched the bedpost once more.

If this was a charade ... no, it wasn't. It couldn't be. Robert would never have allowed it—certainly not one in which he had died. But if it wasn't a charade, what was it? A ruse to keep me from investigating Merton's murder? A hallucination? Whatever this was, I would need to go along with it. It was the only way to discover its meaning and purpose.

Anne's grey eyes softened. "Don't worry, my lady. If you falter, I shall say the fever left you uncertain. None will think it strange."

"The fever?" I echoed faintly.

"Aye. You took poorly not three weeks past. His Majesty himself bade you rest. If your thoughts wander, or if you appear pale, no one will question it. They will think you still weak in body, nothing more." She moved briskly, already reaching for the crimson gown. "We've no time to waste. Her Majesty does not brook delay."

I slipped from the bed, feeling the chill of stone beneath my feet. The bedgown slithered from my shoulders as Anne pressed a linen shift into my hands. It was finer than any chemise I'd ever worn, cool against my skin. Next came the stays, which she laced firmly, muttering apologies at each tug.

"Breathe deeply, my lady—there. You'll stand all the straighter for it."

Before I could protest, she had guided me into petticoats, the rustle of silk whispering in my ears. Then came the gown itself—crimson satin heavy with embroidery, its slashed sleeves revealing glimmers of white beneath. Anne's fingers flew as she fastened hooks and arranged ribbons, stepping back now and again to assess her handiwork.

Once she was done, I glanced down at myself, half-expecting to see me standing in my own room. Instead, I saw a lady of the seventeenth century staring back at me, every inch arrayed for court. Anne knelt to fasten satin shoes upon my feet, their pointed toes peeking from beneath the hem of my gown as though to assure me the transformation was complete.

Having properly shod me, Anne rose and turned her

attention to my hair, dragging a comb through the dark waves with brisk efficiency. She coaxed a few loose curls to frame my face, then bound the rest back with a ribbon of crimson satin to match the gown. A scattering of pearls was pinned among the locks, enough to lend dignity without the elaborate fuss of a banquet coiffure. Finally, she set a narrow strip of lace at the crown so lightly it seemed scarcely to touch.

When she was finished, Anne guided me to a carved walnut table where a tall mirror gleamed within a gilt frame, the glass faintly rippled but clear enough to startle me with its reflection. I hardly recognized the pale woman gazing back. Gone was my 1920s sleekness—the cropped hair tucked beneath a cloche hat, the boyish ease of a straight-cut dress, silk stockings, and simple pumps. In their place stood a seventeenth-century lady swathed in crimson satin, curls adorned with pearls, her narrow waist cinched by stays, her shoes pointed delicately beneath the hem. The stranger in the mirror was elegant, dignified, even prepared for court—yet her eyes betrayed the confusion beneath.

Anne caught my bewildered look and lowered her voice. "Say nothing of it, my lady. You have only to remember you are still recovering from your fever. That will be excuse enough."

I nodded slowly, though my mind reeled. The fever. Yes, best cling to that excuse, for it explained what nothing else could.

Anne set a pearl necklace at my throat and smoothed the satin one last time. "There," she said with satisfaction. "Now come, my lady. We must not keep Queen Catherine waiting."

I followed her toward the door, my steps unsteady, my mind thick with fog. "Anne," I whispered urgently, "forgive me—my thoughts are clouded still. Tell me ... what am I to the queen? What is it I am supposed to do?"

She glanced back, her eyes softening with sympathy. "You are one of Her Majesty's ladies. You attend her, fetch what she requires, and keep her company when she wills it. Naught more demanding than that."

"And if I falter?"

Anne lowered her voice further. "Then I'll say the fever took your memory with it. No one will think it strange, my lady. You are not the first to be struck low and rise again uncertain."

Her words calmed me only a little, yet I clung to them as a drowning woman might a rope. Whatever game this was—dream or madness—I must play my part, and pray my wits held long enough to see me through.

CHAPTER 10

THE QUEEN'S COMPANION

Anne led me from the bedchamber into a corridor lined with paneling so dark it drank the candlelight. We passed through a sequence of passages and galleries, each more bewildering than the last. The ceilings soared above me, painted with mythological scenes that seemed to shift and watch as I walked beneath them. Windows stretched high and narrow, their diamond panes casting fractured light upon the polished floors.

Everywhere, there was movement—pages darting with messages, ladies sweeping past in silks, guards in livery standing rigid at doorways. Voices echoed in a dozen tongues, mingling with the steady creak of boards and the distant notes of a violin drifting from some unseen chamber. I could scarcely take it in. The scale of the place was overwhelming. It felt less like a house and more like a city contained within walls, a maze of chambers and staircases where one could be lost forever.

Anne, brisk and unflustered, guided me down a long gallery hung with tapestries depicting battles I did not recognize. At its end stood a carved doorway draped in heavy velvet, guarded by two men-at-arms with halberds that gleamed in the torchlight. Here, at last, she paused, smoothing her apron and giving me a steadying look.

"Her Majesty waits within," she whispered.

Anne's discreet knock drew an immediate response. The door swung wide, releasing a tide of candlelight and perfume. The withdrawing chamber was warm with fire and roses, a chamber intended for confidences rather than grandeur.

At its center sat the queen—Catherine of Braganza. She was smaller than I imagined. A silver-grey gown enfolded her like mist, a rosary gleamed between her fingers. A lace veil softened the frame of her dark hair, but her eyes—solemn, watchful—pierced the air. She looked serene, but the stillness was strained, as though she endured much and dared not falter.

Two ladies flanked her. One, tall and fair, stood with the stiff hauteur of a woman accustomed to being feared. The other, a younger, round-faced beauty with lively eyes, seemed more anxious to please than to command.

Anne curtsied low. I did my best to follow, only to catch my heel in my skirt. My stumble drew a smirk from the tall blonde, though the younger lady's lips curved in a sympathetic smile.

"You are come at last," Catherine said. Her Portuguese accent softened her words, giving them a lilting, slightly broken rhythm. "I wait and wait. They tell me you are sick. Still with fever?"

I bowed again, my cheeks burning. "Yes, Your Majesty. I am recovering."

Her hand fluttered dismissively. "It is good. You are here. That is enough."

Relief flooded me as she gestured toward a low stool at her side. I obeyed, perching nervously while the blonde lady sniffed faintly.

"You will keep me company," Catherine said, lowering her voice. "I do not like to sit alone with ... gossips." Her eyes flicked toward the blonde, whose expression tightened.

She leaned nearer, her rosary clicking softly. "They speak too much. About me, about my faith, my place. Too much. You—" Her gaze probed mine. "You do not talk."

"No, Your Majesty," I whispered. "Never."

Her lips softened into the faintest smile. "Good. You are friend."

I dared a glance about me, seeing the queen's withdrawing chamber with new eyes. It was not vast like the echoing galleries I had passed through, but intimate, even heavy with presence. Dark oak panels were softened by hangings of crimson velvet worked with golden thread, and the glow of a great hearth painted everything in shifting light. A Turkey carpet muffled footsteps, and stools upholstered in green damask stood waiting for the ladies who lingered at the edges, watchful yet silent.

Above Catherine's chair of state, a canopy fringed with gilt tassels proclaimed her rank, though the crucifix and jeweled rosary in her hands spoke more plainly of her faith. The air was close with the mingled scents of beeswax, rose water, and smoke, and though the chamber was meant for repose, I felt the tension of a place where confidences might be shared—or betrayed.

A cold shiver ran through me. Whatever masquerade or dream I had clung to, it was slipping fast. Hard as it was to believe, I was in the seventeenth century, at the very heart of

Catherine of Braganza's court, and there was no waking from it. But why?

My thoughts flew at once to the murdered antiquarian, to the cryptic manuscript hinting at a conspiracy against the queen. If fate—or madness—had hurled me back here, perhaps it was not an accident at all. Perhaps I had been set down in this world precisely to learn what that manuscript could not tell. Who plotted against Catherine and why?

The danger to me was real enough, but so was the opportunity. If I could endure the charade long enough, I might uncover the truth of a treason whispered three centuries later—and perhaps make sense of Merton's death.

My moment of introspection was broken by the blonde lady who pitched her voice just loudly enough to carry. "Her Majesty grows more fluent each day." She spoke sweetly, but the corners of her mouth curved in a smile that was anything but kind. "Why, soon the court may even follow her prayers in Portuguese."

A ripple of polite laughter stirred among the ladies. Catherine's lips pressed into a thin line, her rosary beads clicking faster between her fingers. She answered in careful English, her accent heavy but her tone sharp. "Better prayers in poor English than sins in perfect speech."

The blonde flushed scarlet but quickly masked it with a brittle laugh.

"Lady Castlemaine," Catherine said flatly, turning away, "tires herself with wit. She thinks she is clever. She is only... tiresome."

Anne leaned close to me, her voice barely above a whisper. "Lady Castlemaine is Her Majesty's Lady of the Bedchamber."

I blinked. If I remembered correctly, Lady Castlemaine had also been the king's mistress.

Anne nodded almost imperceptibly, reading my astonishment. "Aye. His Majesty would have it so, and Her Majesty had no choice but to accept. The appointment was pressed upon her from the first. Castlemaine herself demanded it, and the king insisted. The queen wept and prayed, but in the end she was forced to yield."

I glanced at Catherine, sitting small but straight beneath her canopy of state, her fingers moving restlessly over the rosary. The humiliation must have been galling. Her husband's mistress not merely flaunted in public but installed in her very household, bearing the title of lady of the bedchamber.

Anne's grey eyes narrowed. "And so she struts here as if she were queen herself. It is a cruelty Her Majesty bears every day."

The younger woman leaned close to me with a quick smile. "Her Majesty is well used to such company. Do not let it trouble you."

Anne bent discreetly at my side. "That is Lady Frances Stuart. She is unmarried."

Lady Frances was all soft curves and golden curls, her cheeks prettily flushed, her eyes bright with youth. She could not have been more different from the haughty Castlemaine.

Anne bent a little nearer, her voice a hush meant only for me. "The king dotes upon her—calls her *La Belle Stuart*. Yet she will not yield to him, not even for the crown itself. Many say she guards her virtue more fiercely than a fortress, though she toys with his affection all the same."

So this gentle-faced girl, scarcely older than I, held the king at bay while still enjoying his favor? The thought unsettled me. It spoke of a court where women wielded beauty and wit as weapons and innocence could be turned into a kind of power.

Anne's lips curved faintly, almost proud. "She is the only lady who can check Lady Castlemaine's triumphs. The queen suffers much, but she takes comfort in Lady Frances Stuart, for she vexes the king without ever meaning to."

The name rang through me. Stuart. A coincidence? Or another thread woven into the manuscript's enigma?

Before I could dwell on it, Catherine pressed a folded letter into my hand. The wax seal bore the king's crest. "Read," she said simply.

My stomach dropped. The lines on the page swirled in an elaborate seventeenth-century hand, all flourishes and ink blots. Panic rose hot in my throat.

I fumbled, then lifted my gaze with what I hoped was convincing humility. "Majesty... forgive me. The fever left my sight weak. Perhaps another—"

Her eyes searched mine for a long beat, then shifted to Lady Frances, who took the letter and read it aloud. The contents were banal enough—an account of supplies readied for the Queen's household—but Catherine's fingers tightened on her rosary as though hearing something else beneath the words.

When Frances finished, Catherine dismissed her with a nod but did not release my gaze. "Your eyes will mend. For now, you sit with me. Speak with me. Yes?"

"Yes, Your Majesty," I said.

She leaned closer, her breath carrying the faint scent of cloves. "You are not like the others. You listen." A pause. "I am glad of you."

The words—hesitant, imperfect, but unmistakably sincere—struck me with unexpected force. Here was a queen, lonely in a hostile court, choosing me as confidante. Me, a fraud in borrowed satin.

As I watched them—Catherine small but dignified beneath her canopy, Castlemaine smirking like a cat at the cream, and Frances glowing with youth and untouchable innocence—I felt the threads of a deadly tapestry tightening around the queen. The murdered antiquarian's manuscript had spoken of conspiracy, of treason whispered in dark corners. I did not know who plotted against Catherine of Braganza, or how far the venom reached, but I knew this—I was here for a reason.

Whatever strange fate had carried me into the seventeenth century, it had placed me at the queen's side. And I would not stand idle while she was surrounded by enemies. If I must play the part of a court lady, then so be it. But behind the silks and pearls, my eyes would be sharp and my ears sharper still.

For Catherine's sake, I would find the truth—and make certain no harm came to her.

CHAPTER 11

UNWANTED ADMIRERS

*A*fter some time, the queen dismissed me so she could attend to her private prayers. To my surprise, I found myself swept into the outer chamber, where a dozen courtiers lounged about as though the palace were their private tavern—perfumed with clove-scented smoke, echoing with flirtatious laughter, and glittering with more jewels than a Bond Street window.

I kept close to Anne, hoping to slip quietly away, but it was no use. A pair of young gallants descended at once, all satin and swagger.

"My lady," one drawled, bowing low enough to let his periwig graze the floor. "Word flies faster than pigeons in this palace. Her Majesty favors you. Permit me, then, to offer my own humble service." His eyes, however, strayed not to my face but to the pearls at my throat.

Before I could frame a reply, his companion pressed closer, the scent of cloves and musk nearly overpowering.

"Humble service, bah! What the lady requires is a man of means. I own estates in Kent, and my mother swears there is no finer orchard in England. Come walk with me, and I'll tell you of every apple in it."

I had thought the Restoration court was famed for its elegance. Evidently, it was more fruit market than fairy tale. Pressed between cologne and cloying compliments, I summoned every ounce of my dignity and clutched Anne's arm as though she were a lifeline tossed to a drowning woman. Orchards in Kent indeed. If the man had two thoughts to rub together, they'd both be sticky with pomade.

Anne's elbow found my ribs. "Smile," she hissed.

So I did, though it was closer to a grimace. "How... generous. Alas, I fear I am still recovering from my illness."

The words tasted like chalk, but I delivered them with all the tremulous sweetness of a convalescent lamb. If I'd learned anything from my time in polite society, it was that men like these preferred their women wan and grateful. Or, failing that, too polite to laugh in their faces. My smile wobbled at the corners. But if either of them noticed, they took it for an invitation rather than irony.

"That makes two of us," the orchard-owner purred. "But my remedy is swift—a glass of Canary, taken in pleasant company." He leaned so close I could count the stitches in his embroidered doublet.

Another voice cut through the air. "Stand aside, you jackanapes. You press too near."

The courtiers fell back a step, muttering, as a tall man shouldered through their circle. His skin was bronzed from sun and salt air, his dark hair tied back loosely, his coat plain compared to the peacocks around him. He moved with the easy balance of a sailor more at home on deck than in a gallery.

My breath caught. "Hollingsworth?" The name flew from me before I could stop it.

His head snapped toward me, brows lifting in surprise. For the briefest moment, he looked as startled as I felt.

Of course it was him. Or rather, it should have been. The same angular jaw, the same confident carriage, even the same sardonic gleam in the eye. But the hair was darker, sun-touched and threaded with gray, and he bore the weathered look of a man a decade older than the Hollingsworth I knew. Still, the resemblance was uncanny enough to make my breath hitch. What trick of fate—or bloodline—had placed a man with that face in the court of Charles II? I stared, half-expecting him to vanish like a mirage, and wholly unprepared for the slow, knowing smile that curved across his lips.

"Aye, Edmund Hollingsworth, at your service, madam. Newly come from the Levant." He bowed, eyes glinting with curiosity. "Though I confess myself flattered to be recognized so swiftly."

Heat rushed into my cheeks. "Forgive me. I thought ... I mistook you for someone else.

He arched a brow. "And yet, you knew my name." His smile was quick, edged with curiosity. "Most in this palace scarce recall it, for I've been gone these three years."

The words tangled on my tongue, but I bit them back. *I saw your portrait,* I thought wildly. *Hanging in Hollingsworth House—in my own time.* The pearl glinted now at his ear, the same lustrous drop I had seen framed in oil and gilt. It was impossible, yet here he stood, flesh and blood before me.

The words tangled on my tongue, but the truth slipped out in a rush. "I—I saw your portrait. The earring gave you away."

His gaze lingered on me—steady, searching, as though trying to fit me into a puzzle he hadn't quite assembled. But whatever passed behind his eyes, he masked it with ease.

"Did it?" he murmured. His fingers brushed the pearl that gleamed against his ear—a lustrous drop, the color of moonlight. "A trinket from the Indies, by way of the South Seas. Won off a Dutch prize, and not without risk." He tilted his head slightly. "I must count myself fortunate, to be so memorable."

My pulse fluttered like a trapped bird. The earring, the voice, the infuriating tilt of that smile—it was all so familiar. And yet *he* was not. Older. Weathered by sun and sea. A stranger, and yet not a stranger. I ought to have curtsied, murmured some graceful excuse, and fled. Instead, I stood there gaping like a half-witted milkmaid, my mind scrambling for sense while my feet refused to move.

Then—by some miracle—*he* rescued *me*. He offered his arm with the sort of polished gallantry that came naturally to men who wore swords as easily as smiles. "This chamber is rather thick with perfume, powder, and posturing knaves," he said. "Might I suggest a turn about the gallery instead? I'd very much like to become better acquainted."

For a moment, I hesitated. Every instinct screamed I should keep my distance—from his knowing smile, from this impossible resemblance, from whatever madness had placed me in a world I barely understood.

And yet ... my hand rose of its own accord, settling lightly on his offered arm.

"Very well," I said, schooling my voice to steadiness. "But only a short turn."

A lie, of course. Nothing about this man—or this moment—would prove short.

He steered me away from the press of courtiers, guiding me down a quieter passage where the din of laughter and perfume-drenched boasts faded behind us. His stride was long, unhurried, as though the whole palace belonged to him.

The gallery lay just beyond a pair of carved doors left ajar, opening into a long, high-ceilinged room lined with portraits, tall windows, and shadowed alcoves. Mullioned panes filtered the spring light into slanted bars that striped the floor, catching the gilt edges of frames and the occasional glint of polished armor in a painted scene. Here, the air was cooler and the hush so complete it felt as though the very walls held their breath.

Only a pair of elderly gentlemen sat dozing on a velvet bench at the far end, their wigs askew, leaving the rest of the gallery blessedly empty.

He glanced down at me as we entered the hush of the gallery. "You speak my name with such familiarity," he said, his voice pitched low, meant only for me. "And yet I find myself at a disadvantage—for yours, madam, I do not know."

I drew a steadying breath. "Kathleen Halloran," I said quietly, the name foreign on my tongue. "Widow of Sir Robert Halloran."

His brows lifted. "Ah—Lady Halloran, then." The title rolled easily from his tongue, smooth as aged brandy. But there was a glint beneath it, something sharper, more discerning. "Sir Robert, you say? A fine sailor. I never served under his command, but his name was known in every port and spoken with respect."

The sudden warmth in my chest startled me. For all the falseness of this world. Whatever trick or dream or madness I'd stumbled into, Anne's grief earlier, and now this man's quiet reverence made Robert's death feel real. Real enough to ache.

His smile softened. "And the widow of Sir Robert Halloran holds the Queen's favor. That explains why every jackanapes in Whitehall is buzzing about you."

A prickle ran across my skin. "I do not seek theirs." The last thing I wished was to call attention to myself. I'd be perfectly happy disappearing into the wainscoting.

He lifted a hand, palm outward, forestalling my protest. "Do not be alarmed. When a queen singles out a lady, the whole palace takes note. It is nothing more mysterious than gossip doing its work. But fear not." His voice dropped, low and steady. "Not every ear at Whitehall delights in mischief. Some of us would rather keep a confidence than trade it."

His words steadied me, though unease lingered. Could I truly trust him? I had already betrayed myself once by blurting his name. If he pressed further, if he guessed too much, heaven help me.

"Mm." He let me off the hook with a half-smile, as though filing the matter away for later. "A man could do worse than be called upon by such a wonderful lady, especially when she did it with such urgency." He tilted his head. "Shall I take it, then, that you wish to be friends?"

The steadiness in his gaze disarmed me. Despite the foreign cut of his coat and the air of salt and distance about him, there was something in his manner that felt ... familiar.

"Yes," I said softly, surprised at how much I meant it. "Friends."

He offered a small bow of acknowledgment, more sincere than courtly. "Then you may count on me, my lady. These halls are full of wolves in satin, and a lone dove makes easy prey. Better you have an old sailor at your side than none at all."

I managed a laugh, faint but real, as tension unwound in my chest. For the first time since I had awakened in this bewildering century, I did not feel entirely alone.

I clutched his arm, my heart still pounding. He didn't know me. Not the way the Hollingsworth of my own world did. And yet he played his part as though we shared an understanding, slipping into the ruse with the grace of a practiced actor.

"Lady Halloran." Catherine's steward appeared suddenly,

a severe man in plain black, his eyes hard as flint. "Her Majesty requires your presence."

"Yes, of course." I turned to my new friend. "Forgive me, Lord Hollingsworth."

His eyes flickered with … something. Amusement, perhaps. Or curiosity. I could not tell. Before I could puzzle it out, he bowed smoothly and kissed my hand, a twinkle in his eyes. "Until next time, my lady."

The steward glared at him until he let me go.

I followed the steward back to the withdrawing room with Anne trailing behind. My heart still hammered when the door shut close.

"The courtiers circle like crows," Anne muttered, tugging my sleeve straight. "Best keep your wits, my lady. Some seek favor, some seek fortune. But all will take what they can."

Her words chilled me more than the suitors' advances. If I were to survive in this court, I would need more than borrowed satin and a fever-borne excuse. I would need allies, and I would need them quickly.

"What about Hollingsworth?"

She didn't hesitate. "Keep him close. A man like that—steady, sharp, and not dazzled by silk and titles—you'll not find many of his sort here."

I nodded, though a hundred questions still tangled in my mind. He wasn't my Hollingsworth. But there was strength in him, and kindness, too, hidden beneath the salt and steel. In a world where everything felt unfamiliar, he was the closest thing to solid ground.

And for now, that would have to be enough.

CHAPTER 12

MURMURS OF TREASON

*A*fter the queen, pleading weariness, dismissed her attendants early that evening, Anne guided me from the withdrawing chamber into the long gallery beyond, where the air was cooler and the rushlights guttered in their sconces.

How different the gallery seemed now. With Hollingsworth beside me it had felt almost a refuge, the hush companionable. Tonight, stripped of his presence, the silence pressed like a weight, broken only by whispers sharp enough to cut.

A group of courtiers lingered near the windows, their laughter hushed, as though secrecy were a sweeter wine than the claret in their goblets.

As we neared, one of the men broke away and bowed with a mocking flourish. His satin sleeves brushed the floor as a jeweled pomander swung at his waist. "The queen's new pet," he said in a voice loud enough to carry. "Tell us, sweet dove, do you whisper in Her Majesty's ear as she prays to Rome?"

I froze, my pulse hammering, even as laughter rippled through the knot of men.

Anne tugged my sleeve. "Best we pass quickly, my lady."

But I lingered, drawn by the low murmur of voices—a sound less like conversation and more like conspiracy. The other men stood close together, their powdered heads bowed, shadows flickering across their faces in the wavering light.

Whispered snippets reached my ears.

"...she weakens him, the Portuguese witch..."

"...the Queen bears no sons—nor daughters either."

"A barren womb is no foundation for England's crown."

"...Arlington has the papers—sealed under the rose..."

"...ships at Dover...a bargain struck..."

"...the King blind as ever, too besotted to see..."

Each phrase reached me in tatters, carried on the breath of wine and malice, but together they painted a picture that chilled my blood.

Another voice, smoother, edged with pride: "There are maids of Protestant virtue enough—one nearer than most would guess. A girl fair, obedient, bred to please a king. My own would serve England better than any Portuguese papist."

A murmur of approval followed, low and dangerous, like the rustle of silk over steel.

"Speak softer," another hissed. "Walls have ears."

I schooled my features to bland disinterest, though inside my thoughts raced. Arlington—the name rang in my ears, tethered to some half-formed memory I could not yet place. I glimpsed a folded parchment passed from hand to hand, caught the phrase *sealed under the rose*, a murmur of ships. And then—darker still—they spoke of the Queen's barrenness, of replacing her. My blood chilled. There was only one way to unseat a queen. She would have to die.

A tall man with a hawkish nose turned sharply, caught me staring, and narrowed his eyes.

Anne pulled harder, her voice tight. "Come, my lady. There's no safety in lingering here."

This time, I let her lead me on, though my mind stayed rooted to that shadowed corner of the gallery, where secrets simmered beneath the surface like embers waiting for breath.

Our skirts whispered along the floor as we quickened our pace, but their words clung to me like smoke. *Papers. Ships at Dover. A bargain struck. The Queen's barrenness."*

Those very phrases might be written in the murdered antiquarian's manuscript.

Anne led me to the small chamber allotted to me and barred the door firmly behind us. Her face was pale in the rushlight. "Mind this, my lady, you hear much at court, but you speak of nothing. Promise me."

I nodded, though my voice trembled and my thoughts clamored otherwise. "I promise." After a pause, I added, "But who were those men? The one with the hawkish nose. He looked at me as though I had already betrayed him."

Anne hesitated, her hand tightening on the latch. "Sir John Denham," she said at last. "The others were Edward Montagu, Sir William Coventry, and Henry Jermyn. All of them cleverer with their tongues than wise with their souls. And all of them dangerous."

"The names mean little to me," I admitted. "Are they important enough to direct such efforts toward the Queen?"

Anne's mouth tightened. "Important enough to lend weight but not to lead. Men such as these follow another's banner. A greater lord sets them whispering, and they are glad to carry his words."

I pressed her. "Their words hinted at some conspiracy. I heard enough to know it was more than idle talk."

Her eyes darted to the door, though it was barred fast. "That I cannot tell you. Not because I would not, but because to speak of it is peril itself. Best you forget what scraps you caught."

But forgetting was impossible. The names burned in my mind, and with them the fragments of treasonous whispers. Arlington. Dover. Sealed under the rose. And, most assuredly, a conspiracy against Her Majesty.

Anne turned away, busying herself with the tinderbox, coaxing a spark to the waiting candlewick. "Trust me, my lady. The less you know, the safer you are."

Safer, perhaps, but no wiser. And wisdom, I thought grimly, might be the only thing to keep me alive in Whitehall.

Yet even as I lay that night beneath heavy damask curtains, I knew silence would not be enough. If treason stalked the queen, I was already caught in its snare.

CHAPTER 13

FOLLOWING THE CLUES

Sleep proved impossible. The courtiers' whispers haunted me, twining with memories of the murdered antiquarian and his cryptic manuscript. *Papers... proofs... a scheme to cast aside the queen.*

By morning, my resolve had hardened. If I were to endure this strange masquerade, I must do more than curtsy and smile. I had to investigate.

Anne fussed with my gown as we prepared to attend the queen. "Keep your eyes low, my lady. It is safest."

Safe. The word clung like dust. Anne meant well, trying to shield me with obedience and silence, but it was not in my nature to look down and walk past danger. Not when whispers of plots coiled through these gilded halls, not when a queen's life might hang in the balance. I had to look closer. I had to know.

I caught her hand. "Anne, if there is danger to Her Majesty, I cannot look away."

Her grey eyes flicked to mine, troubled but loyal. She said nothing more, though her silence was answer enough.

The day unfolded in a blur of duties—handing the queen her embroidery silks, holding a basin for her ablutions, listening as she murmured prayers in Portuguese. The other ladies watched me with suspicion, especially Lady Castlemaine, who lingered like a cat waiting to pounce.

By early afternoon, Her Majesty declared herself weary of close air and candle smoke. "A little sun, a little breeze," she said softly, her Portuguese accent lilting. "Come, Lady Halloran, you will attend me."

Grateful for the errand, I followed as we descended to the garden walks. The air was temperate, touched with the faintest edge of autumn. Roses still bloomed, their perfume mingling with the damp scent of clipped yew.

But scarcely had we begun our promenade when the King himself appeared, striding toward us with two gentlemen in tow. The courtiers melted back with bows, leaving him space.

Charles Stuart was taller than I expected, his dark hair tumbling loose about his shoulders, his long face made striking by a hooked nose and quick, searching eyes. There was an ease in his gait, a restless energy in every movement, as though he could never stand still long enough to be pinned down. He smiled often, but the smile sat crooked on his lips—half-mockery, half-mirth, revealing little of what he truly thought.

At his side walked Lord Hollingsworth—tall, bronzed, his plain coat a stark contrast to the satin peacocks cluttering Whitehall.

"Madam," the King said, bowing over the Queen's hand. "I crave but a moment's private word."

Catherine inclined her head, serene but wary.

Charles glanced past her to me. "Lady Halloran, you will

forgive me if I steal Her Majesty from your company. But I shall not leave you unattended." His eyes slid toward his companion with a wry smile. "Hollingsworth, see that our lady does not lose her way."

The command was light, almost careless, but it set my pulse racing all the same.

Hollingsworth bowed while offering me a half-smile. "It would be my honor."

Charles tucked the Queen's hand into the crook of his arm and drew her a few paces aside, their voices dropping to a murmur beneath the rustle of the yews. I could not hear the words, but I saw Catherine's gaze lift to his with quiet intensity. The King's expression shifted between impatience and amusement, like a man indulging a favorite hound.

For a moment, I felt the strangeness of it all press close—the queen of England confiding her heart to her notorious husband, while I, Kitty Worthington of Eaton Square, stood disguised as her attendant in a century not my own.

A low voice intruded on my thoughts. "Best let them be," Hollingsworth said, falling into step beside me. "The King does not relish an audience when he feigns attentiveness."

I turned toward him, the sun catching the silver threaded through his dark hair. He smiled faintly, offering his arm. "Since His Majesty commands it, we must walk. Though I admit, I do not find the prospect disagreeable."

I laid my hand lightly on his arm, grateful for the steadiness of his presence. For a few moments we walked in silence, the gravel crunching beneath our steps, the air fragrant with late roses. The King's laughter drifted faintly from behind the clipped hedges, brittle as glass.

"I am glad it is you," I said at last, my voice low.

He arched a brow. "Glad, madam?"

"That His Majesty appointed you to walk with me. There

are … few others I would trust." In reality, there was no other.

His eyes flicked to mine, quick and shrewd. "Trust is a costly gift in this place. Are you certain you wish to spend it on me?"

I drew a careful breath. "Last night, in the gallery, I heard things. Whispers not meant for my ears."

He did not start, nor even slow his stride, but I felt the subtle shift in him, the way a man at sea braces when he scents a storm.

"And what did these whispers speak of?" he asked softly.

"Ships. Papers. A bargain struck. And …" I hesitated, the words chilling me even now. "The Queen."

The gravel crunched louder in the hush that followed, as though the garden itself were holding its breath.

Hollingsworth's gaze stayed forward, his expression smooth, but his voice was low and taut. "You've stepped into peril, Lady Halloran. Words like those—spoken too freely—could cost a life."

My stomach tightened. "Then you believe I heard aright?"

"I believe," he said carefully, "that you should not carry such knowledge alone." At last, he looked at me, his eyes intent. "Meet me after the banquet this evening. There is a small, cloistered walk beyond the chapel where we may speak without fear of listening ears."

He offered no smile now, only the faintest dip of his head, as though sealing a pact. "Until then, keep your face serene, and your tongue still. Trust me to do the rest."

Before I could answer, a voice rang across the garden. "Hollingsworth!"

The King beckoned, his tone warm with satisfaction. The Queen stood beside him, her expression unreadable in the dappled light.

As we reached him, Charles spread his arms in a gesture half-magnanimous, half-theatrical. "My good Sir Edmund has served me well, and I will not have his loyalty go unrewarded. From this day, he is no longer merely a knight of my realm, but ennobled as the first Marquis of Hollingsworth, with an estate to match."

A murmur rippled through the attendants. Charles seized Hollingsworth's hand and raised it high as though presenting a champion to the lists, then turned to the gathered courtiers with a crooked smile. "Mark him well, gentlemen. England has few such servants, and fewer still as faithful. A Dutch flagship taken, an English squadron plucked from ruin. Such deeds are not soon forgotten."

The courtiers bowed deeper, voices buzzing with congratulations that could not conceal the edge of envy. I caught a hissed whisper behind me: "From sailor to marquis in a single breath... "

Hollingsworth inclined his head, accepting the honor with the steady composure of a man long accustomed to storms.

The King clapped him on the shoulder. "You may not enjoy your lands much, as you'll be needed at sea again soon enough. But you'll leave behind an heir, eh? Best find a wife before the tide turns. England can ill afford to lose men of your mettle."

Hollingsworth's smile was faint, fleeting, his eyes unreadable. I could not tell if he heard in the King's words command, jest, or warning.

But my own heart jolted. *The first Marquis Hollingsworth*. I was standing at the very moment the title was born, watching history etch itself into the man who bore the face of the one I knew.

And yet the King's final words echoed louder than the rest. *Best find a wife ... leave behind an heir*.

Who would he choose? Which woman would claim his hand, his name, his future?

The question lingered long after the garden fell silent.

CHAPTER 14

THE QUEEN'S PERIL

After the King took his leave, much pleased with himself, Her Majesty expressed a wish to attend her prayers. Again. I was becoming rapidly acquainted with her habit of constant devotion. Small wonder she sought solace at the altar, given the King's predilections.

In her place, I might have arranged for Lady Castlemaine's swift banishment and slept soundly thereafter. But I was no royal personage, and I came from another century altogether. Catherine had neither freedom of thought nor action. Prayer was the one refuge still permitted her.

Thus it was that Anne and I followed in her train to the chapel, the air growing cooler as we passed from the lamp-lit corridors into the hush of incense and candle smoke.

The palace chapel was dim that evening, its stone walls hushed with incense and shadow. Catherine knelt long in prayer, her veil trembling slightly with each whispered word. The other ladies lingered dutifully behind her, though Castlemaine smothered a yawn with jeweled fingers.

When the Queen at last rose, her attendants gathered close, ready to sweep her away to her chambers. I moved to follow, unwilling to let her out of my sight.

But Catherine turned to me, her hand briefly alighting on mine. In a low voice, meant for me alone, she said, "You should rest before supper, my lady. I would not have you faint from fatigue at table." Then, after the briefest pause, she leaned nearer, her dark eyes intent. "It is a dangerous thing to be alone in this world. You should consider a new husband. A worthy one."

My breath caught, but before I could frame a reply, she was gone—swept down the passage by her Portuguese attendants, her veil a pale banner trailing after her.

I lingered a moment longer, drawn by the play of candlelight on the carved altar.

Suddenly, a man materialized seemingly from the shadows near the sacristy door—a priest, robed in black, his tonsured head bowed. "You should not tarry alone." His accent was Portuguese, his English careful and uneven, like Catherine's.

The voice startled me. "I beg your pardon, Father," I stammered.

He inclined his head. "No pardon needed. Only ... caution." His eyes, dark and anxious, flicked to the empty doorway where the Queen had vanished. "You are close to Her Majesty now. You must be eyes, ears. You must protect her."

I swallowed hard. I already sought to do that. Given his advice, he probably had more information than I did. "Protect her? From whom?"

His gaze sharpened. "From those who would see her dead. There are whispers—papers circulate, men gather in secret. They speak not only of sending her away but of ending her life. Her Catholic faith is cause enough for them to hate."

My heart thudded so loud I feared Anne could hear it. "You are certain?"

"Certain," he said grimly. "Too many times I have heard it in confession, cloaked as idle fancy, but the venom is real. One day, poison in her cup or a dagger at her breast. It is not if, but when."

The words chilled me to the bone.

Anne made the sign of the cross swiftly, whispering, "God preserve her."

The priest pressed a hand to his breast. "Tell her nothing yet. She bears enough grief. But watch. Listen. Bring word to me if you hear more. I will know how to place it in safer hands."

And with that, he melted back into the shadows, leaving only the faint echo of his warning.

I stood rooted to the flagstones, trembling. Whispers of treason had become a prophecy of murder.

Anne touched my arm gently. "What will you do, my lady?"

A fair question. I forced myself to breathe, though the air tasted of ash. What power had I to keep the Queen safe? I had no authority here, no trusted position. I was neither spy nor soldier. I was only a lady pressed into service, my presence tolerated but not welcome. Yet I could not—would not —do nothing.

I thought of the ways one might protect a queen without ever drawing a blade. Watch the servants. Mark the dishes as they were brought forward. Note who lingered too near her cup, who whispered too intently at her shoulder, who pressed her to eat or drink. The danger might come from without or within, from enemy or supposed friend.

We left the chapel in silence, Anne guiding me toward my assigned bedchamber. Chilled as I was from the incense-laden air and cold flagstones, I welcomed the heat cast by the fire burning in the hearth.

Anne set to work at once, loosening the ribbons of my day dress with deft fingers. I stood rigid beneath her touch, my mind still replaying the priest's warning: *poison in her cup ... a dagger at her breast.*

After she drew the gown from my shoulders, she poured rose-scented water into a shallow basin and wrung out a linen cloth. "Here, my lady. Just a quick refresh before you take your rest."

She pressed the cool cloth gently to my face, then passed it over my neck and hands. The faint fragrance of roses soothed me, though it did little to ease the weight of the priest's warning in my thoughts. When she turned away, I finished the task myself, dabbing discreetly at the places no maid need attend. It was a small relief to feel clean.

Following the Queen's advice, I took my rest and soon drifted into sleep. What felt like mere minutes later, Anne's voice roused me. "Come, my lady—it is time to dress."

She slipped a cool linen chemise over my head. Then came the new attire: a gown of pale ivory silk, its square neckline edged with delicate lace, the skirts embroidered with sprays of silver thread. Anne fastened the stomacher with quick, precise hands, then drew a sash of deep blue satin about my waist.

After stepping back to survey her work, she guided me toward the tall mirror set above the dressing table. "Sit, my lady," she murmured, reaching for the jeweled box at hand.

I obeyed, lowering myself onto the cushioned stool. I stared down at myself as though at a stranger. How strange, to dress for splendor while thinking only of peril. The jewels

Anne clasped at my throat gleamed cold as chains. The pearls she pinned in my hair might as well have been drops of ice.

Still, I reminded myself, appearances at court were armor of their own. If I could not wield a blade, I would wear my beauty as a shield, my eyes as weapons sharp enough to pierce deceit. I would watch. I would listen. I would protect the Queen, whatever it cost me.

"You look radiant, my lady."

I forced a smile. "Then let us pray the light blinds our enemies before they strike."

If I had no sword, then I would make my eyes my sharpest weapon.

Anne gave me a worried glance. "You are pale."

"Too much incense," I murmured, though we both knew it was more than that.

A knock came at the chamber door, and a young page bowed his head inside. "Her Majesty prepares to enter the banquet hall. You are wanted, my lady."

I rose at once, smoothing the silk skirts that still felt more like armor than adornment, and followed Anne back through the corridors.

When the Queen emerged at last from her chambers, dressed in a gown of dark blue satin trimmed with pearls, I felt my stomach knot. She smiled faintly, but the sight gave me little comfort. Her very serenity seemed proof she suspected nothing of the venom brewing around her.

As we proceeded along the corridors to the banquet hall, the sound of viols and trumpets carried to us, along with the heady scent of roasted meats. Yet for me, the feast ahead was no celebration. It was a battlefield, and every dish a weapon waiting to be wielded.

The hall glittered with candlelight, silver chargers, and covered platters gleaming upon the long tables, while the restless murmur of courtiers eager for diversion mingled with the strains of music that filled the pause. Her Majesty took her place at the high table, her ladies gathered near, yet not a morsel was touched. All eyes turned expectantly to the great doors.

At last, they opened, and the King entered to a swell of music and the rustle of silks as the company rose in unison. Charles looked pleased with the spectacle, acknowledging bows and curtsies with a languid smile before taking his seat beside the Queen. Only then did the meal begin.

For me, the splendor blurred into menace. Each goblet poured might carry death. Each dish set before Her Majesty might conceal poison. I watched Catherine as closely as a hawk—her delicate hands lifting a cup, her lips touching the rim. My breath caught until she set it down again. A moment later, she sampled a morsel of fish, and my pulse hammered, waiting for her to falter, to pale, to fall. She did not.

I took some comfort in noting that her wine was drawn from the same decanter as the King's, her food served from the same platters placed before him. Yet if treachery came, it would be Catherine's cup singled out, her portion marked. She alone was the target.

From just behind my chair, Anne murmured a quiet prayer, the words scarcely reaching my ears. Across the table, Castlemaine's mocking eyes caught mine, as though she guessed my terror and delighted in it. The courtiers laughed, jested, raised their glasses. I saw only peril.

At one point a servant stumbled, spilling wine across the rushes. The hall erupted in laughter, but I nearly leapt to my feet, certain it was some signal, some stratagem. Yet nothing followed—only red stains seeping into straw.

The banquet dragged on, course after glittering course. My stomach turned from dread. Though food enough was placed before me, I ate little. Each moment stretched, weighted with fear. But at last, the Queen rose, smiling faintly, her health intact. The courtiers bowed, the music swelled, and she departed unharmed.

Relief left me weak, but not reassured. The priest's words clung to me like smoke—*not if, but when*.

As the hall began to empty, I lingered at the edge of the crowd, heart still hammering. No sooner had I drawn a steadying breath than a young courtier with carefully curled hair and a smile too polished for sincerity bowed low before me.

"My lady, you honor Whitehall with your presence. Might I escort you to the next dance?" His eyes gleamed with something more than courtesy. Speculation, perhaps? Or calculation.

Before I could fashion a reply, another gentleman pressed nearer, murmuring his name and offering a compliment so florid I scarcely heard it. Their eagerness unsettled me as much as the banquet had. I could not imagine why they should seek my company with such sudden ardor.

From just behind me, Anne leaned close and whispered, "Plead a headache, my lady."

I touched my brow, letting my shoulders sink as though weary. "You do me much honor, sirs," I said, forcing a faint smile. "But the incense of the chapel has left me with a dreadful headache. I must beg to retire."

The disappointment in the courtiers' faces was plain, but I made my curtsy and slipped from their hopeful gazes into the corridor beyond. Anne fell into step beside me as we wound our way back toward my bedchamber, the hush of the passage a blessed relief after the press of the hall.

"Why do they come at me so avidly?" I asked under my breath. "I have done nothing to encourage them."

Anne gave a small, knowing smile. "They see you as a prize to be won, my lady. Beauty, grace, and a place near the Queen. It is enough to whet any man's appetite."

Her words unsettled me, though I could not fathom what they truly meant. A prize? I quickly dismissed it. There was no time to dwell on such riddles.

Once inside my chamber, I turned to Anne. "I am to meet Lord Hollingsworth in the cloistered walk. There are matters we must discuss privately. You must not wait up for me."

Anne's eyes widened for only a heartbeat, then she inclined her head, as calm as if I had told her I meant to take the air. "Then you shall need a shawl. It is cold in the cloistered walk."

She drew a dark wrap from the press and settled it about my shoulders, her hands lingering a moment in quiet benediction. I managed a faint smile of thanks before slipping out the door.

CHAPTER 15

WHISPERS IN THE CLOISTERED SHADOWS

The cloistered walk lay in half-darkness, its stone arches silvered by moonlight, its flagstones leeching chill through the soles of my slippers. A draught wound along the passage like a ghostly hand, carrying with it the faint strains of music from the hall. I drew my shawl closer about my shoulders, grateful for its thin warmth. No sensible courtier would choose such a place for a tryst, not when warm galleries and lamplit chambers stood ready. This was no lovers' haunt. It was cold, silent, and watchful—an ideal place for secrets.

Hollingsworth stood beneath one of the arches, his face caught in a pale shaft of moonlight, his broad shoulders half in shadow. The merriment of the banquet clung no longer to him. He looked grave, intent, as though he too felt the weight of what had passed this night. When his gaze found mine, something flickered in his eyes—recognition, perhaps, or relief. The quickness of my step betrayed how much I had longed to see him.

"You came," he said softly.

"How could I not?" My voice was steadier than I felt, echoing against the stones as I moved closer. "There is much you must hear."

His eyes searched mine. "There is something new?"

I nodded, pulling the shawl tighter about my shoulders.

He glanced past me toward the arcade, his expression sharpening. "Wait here a moment."

Before I could ask why, he strode the length of the cloister, his boots sounding low against the flagstones. He moved with a soldier's economy, pausing at each arch to peer into the darkness beyond. At the far end he vanished into shadow, then returned, his cloak stirring faintly in the draught.

"No one," he said when he reached me again, lowering his voice. "We are alone. Now tell me, what have you learned?"

"In the chapel tonight, after prayers, a priest stopped me. He said he had heard it too many times in confession to dismiss as rumor—poison in her cup, or a dagger at her breast. He told me it was not if but when."

Hollingsworth's mouth tightened. "Then the danger is nearer than even I feared."

"You feared it already?"

"After leaving the King's presence tonight, I was pulled aside by two men I trust. Old friends. They've heard the talk spreading through Whitehall and London alike. The whispers are no longer confined to idle gossip. Pamphlets pass from hand to hand—venomous things likening Catherine to Jezebel, calling her a foreign infection to be cut away. And it is not just scribblers. Members of Parliament mutter openly of removing her. Some call it exile. Others ..." His jaw tightened. "Others call it justice by steel or poison."

My breath caught.

He studied me gravely. "There is bluster—drunkards in

taverns, like Sir Geoffrey Markham, boasting of daggers after too much claret. Such men are cowards. But there are names I take seriously. Sir Thomas Overton, a Puritan voice in Parliament, is one. And Lord Gabriel Parquier. He has both influence and the purse to hire men who do not flinch at murder. When their names appear in the same breath as pamphlets, I take heed."

A chill swept through me, though the air was already cold. "Then the priest spoke truth. It is not if, but when."

"It is." He lowered his tone further. "But the King hears the whispers and laughs them off. Charles believes his charm is enough to silence hatred. But hatred has sharper teeth than wit can blunt."

I pressed a hand against the cold stone of the pillar beside me. "Then she truly is in peril."

"She is," he agreed, his eyes never leaving mine.

"But what can we do?" The words tumbled out sharper than I intended.

If I had been in my own time, I would have known exactly what to do—investigate, identify suspects, and ask questions until the truth slipped free. But this was not my time. Here, one false step could hurl me into peril. If memory served, they thought nothing of chopping off heads in this century—one careless word branded treason. And though the great witch trials were waning, women who spoke too boldly, or knew too much, might still be whispered of as witches. The thought made me draw my shawl closer, as though its thin folds could shield me.

"There are many things we can do," Hollingsworth said slowly, his voice steady as the stone beneath our feet. He paused then, his gaze sharpening as it fixed upon me, as though he meant to pierce through every layer of disguise I wore.

"But before we speak of any of them," he continued at last,

his tone low and deliberate, "there is something I must know."

A chill stole through me, though the draught had never ceased along the cloister.

"The portrait you claimed to have seen," he said, each word deliberate, "does not exist. I have never sat for one. And the pearl earring you noted with such certainty—" He touched his ear, where the jewel glimmered faintly in the moonlight. "I acquired it only months ago while I was away from the court. It could never have appeared in a likeness."

My throat tightened, the cold air rasping in my lungs.

"Nor am I the man you called me. Until this day, I bore no title but Sir Edmund Hollingsworth, a mere knight. Only by the King's hand was I raised to a marquis this afternoon." He leaned closer, his eyes unflinching. "So tell me, Lady Halloran, how did you know me at once? You looked at me as one greets an old acquaintance. Yet, we had never before set eyes upon each other."

His words struck like hammer blows. I had thought my explanations clever enough—that a slip of the tongue here, a feigned memory there, might carry me through. But I had not counted on time itself betraying me. He had indeed had his portrait painted, but not yet. He had acquired the pearl, but only months ago. And I had addressed him as a lord before the King had bestowed the title. Heaven only knew how many more such mistakes I would make. No matter how careful I was, I was bound to stumble. And each stumble brought me closer to ruin.

"Who are you?" he asked, voice low but inexorable. "Tell me truly. I have traveled far and seen marvels beyond counting—wonders and terrors enough that little could astonish me now. Whatever truth you hold, I will not be driven from you by it."

The arches loomed about me, stone and shadow pressing close.

I closed my eyes for a moment, summoning courage. Heaven help me, the truth was too wild to be believed. Yet to say nothing would condemn me more surely.

"You are right," I said at last, my voice no more than a whisper. "I knew you without ever having met you. Because I come … not from here. Not from now. From another time altogether."

His gaze sharpened. "Another time?"

"The future," I forced out. My breath caught, but the words spilled on. "I live in the year 1925. I saw your portrait once, hanging in a . . . gallery. I couldn't very well tell him it was at his descendant's home. I knew you from that likeness—the same eyes, the same bearing. That is how I recognized you."

Silence pressed between us, heavy as stone.

At length, he tilted his head. "A clever tale. And yet …" His eyes searched mine, as if weighing not the words but the conviction behind them. "There is more. You tell me of portraits and centuries yet to come, but I know when a story is half-told. There is something you keep back."

My pulse thundered. Of course I kept it back. I could not tell him the whole—could not risk unraveling the future that bore his name, nor endanger the very man I had known in my own century. If he thought me mad, so be it. Better madness than the annihilation of his line.

"I have told you the truth," I said, though my voice shook.

Hollingsworth studied me for a long moment. Then, to my astonishment, he gave the faintest smile. "You are unlike any woman I have ever met, Lady Halloran. Perhaps even unlike any woman in this world. I will not press you further tonight. But know this—whatever else you conceal, I will find it out."

I swallowed hard, fearing what he might uncover, yet some part of me warmed at his words. For all his disbelief, he had not turned from me.

"We cannot waste time," I said, forcing steadiness into my voice. "If what you have heard is true, and what I was told tonight as well, the Queen may already be in mortal danger."

"What are you planning to do?" he asked.

"I must warn her," I said at last, lifting my chin. "Not with wild tales, but plain advice. She should take food and drink only from those she trusts—the attendants who came with her from Portugal. At least then the risk of poison would be lessened. And all else—the preparation of her dishes, the pouring of her wine—must be watched with care."

Hollingsworth regarded me steadily. "Sensible counsel. She is more likely to heed it if it comes from a woman she trusts. But how would you approach Her Majesty?"

"I will ask to speak to her quietly," I said. "Better she think me over scrupulous than suffer for my silence."

A faint smile touched his lips. "You are bold, Lady Halloran. Bolder than most men at court. Very well. Warn her, but guard your own steps as closely as you would hers."

"What will you do?" I asked.

Hollingsworth inclined his head. "I will keep my eyes upon the men who spread this venom—Overton, Parquier, their creatures—and learn what I can. My friends at court still trust me. And in taverns and coffeehouses, tongues wag more freely than they should. If there is to be a strike, I mean to hear of it before it falls."

His gaze softened. "Between us, we may yet keep Catherine safe. But it will require silence, patience, and no small amount of cunning. Are you willing?"

"I am," I said, though my heart hammered. Already I feared the risk. To caution Catherine directly was no small step. One word misplaced, one glance observed, and the

Queen's kindness toward me might be twisted into suspicion. Worse still, wagging tongues could turn my warning into gossip. And gossip in Whitehall could be as deadly as any blade.

"Then we are agreed," he answered gravely. "You guard the Queen at her table, and I will hunt her enemies in the shadows. And know this—" his hand brushed mine briefly, deliberately "—I will not see harm come to you either."

For a long moment we stood in the silence of the cloister, the chill air coiling between us like a vow. Then Hollingsworth reached for my hand—not in courtly show, but with the sure clasp of a comrade. His fingers were warm against mine, steadying, binding. Moonlight silvered the arches and caught the dark gleam of his eyes as he held my gaze. "Together, then," he said softly.

A dangerous warmth stirred in me, answering his. Here, in this strange century, I had found an ally—and more than that, perhaps a kindred spirit. Yet even as the thought quickened my pulse, another shadow rose—Robert. I could almost see him pacing Eaton Square, searching for me, frantic for word. If I were hurt—or worse—he would be beside himself. The knowledge twisted inside me, leaving me torn between the man before me and the one I had left behind.

CHAPTER 16

A FATAL FALL

*S*leep was hard to come by that night, a fragile thing that hovered just out of reach. Hollingsworth's words, the priest's warning, the memory of the Queen's serene face—all wove themselves into a restless tangle, leaving me dozing rather than dreaming. When at last slumber caught me, it was shallow, easily broken.

Through the mist of that half-sleep, a voice reached me—Robert's voice, raw with grief.

"Come back to me, Catherine. Please ... come back to me." The anguish in his tone was unbearable, every word weighted with sorrow. *"I cannot lose you. I will not let death claim you."*

I jolted awake with tears upon my cheeks, his plea echoing through me. What was happening to me in 1925? If I lay unconscious, how long could I remain so before my body faltered? How long before Robert's fears became truth? I had to return. I had to find a way back. But how? The question pressed upon me like the stones of the cloister itself, heavy, unyielding, offering no answer.

"My lady!"

Anne's urgent whisper snapped me upright. She stood at my bedside, her cheeks pale, her hands clutched tight around her rosary. Her gaze fell upon my face, stricken. "You were weeping in your sleep."

I touched my cheek, still damp. "A bad dream. That is all," I whispered, though the ache in my chest told me it was far more than that.

Her gaze lingered on me, full of sorrow. "I am sorry to wake you to yet more grief ... but I fear I must."

My throat tightened as I forced myself to meet her eyes. "What is it?"

"One of Her Majesty's attendants—Lady Margaret Elwood. They found her this morning, at the bottom of the back stair near the buttery." Anne's voice faltered, her fingers knotting tighter around the beads. "She is dead."

Cold swept me more surely than the draught in the room.

The name stirred only a faint impression—one of the many young women who drifted like shadows in the Queen's train. Fair hair, perhaps? I had spoken with her once. But she did have a bright spark in her eyes when she lingered near the Queen's circle and had been quick to offer some tidbit of gossip and opinion. She'd struck me as young, ambitious, and eager to be noticed. The thought of her lying broken at the foot of some dark stair hollowed my chest. No matter her temperament, her death must be investigated.

"How did she die?"

"They say she fell." Anne swallowed. "Others claim she was seen drinking too much mead last night. Or wine. That she lost her footing in the dark."

In 1925, no coroner worth his salt would rest on idle talk and rumor. Cause of death demanded facts, not whispers in corridors. If she had fallen, had anyone seen it? If she had drunk too much, who had given her the wine?

"Was she alone? Did someone see her fall?"

Anne appeared somewhat confused by my question. "I know not, my lady."

Clearly, I would not get any more facts from her. She was only repeating what others said. I needed to discover the truth for myself. And that meant, at the very least, inspecting the place where Lady Margaret had fallen.

"Help me dress so I can ascertain the truth for myself."

Anne's gaze flicked to me, startled by the sharpness in my tone, the sudden resolve. "My lady ... you must be careful," she whispered.

Sage advice. One I doubted I would follow. With her help, I dressed in haste, my mind tumbling with questions that rose faster than I could voice them. Why that stair, near the buttery of all places? What had drawn her there in the first place—a lover, or something else altogether?

The corridors were already astir when we stepped into them. Clusters of courtiers lingered in corners, their whispers sharp as the snap of dry twigs. Faces turned as I passed —some pale with fear, others alight with morbid curiosity. From the far end of the gallery came the hushed words *accident* and *fall*, chased quickly by darker murmurs of *murder*.

I reached the stair to find a crowd had gathered, their whispers eddying like smoke:

"She was ever reckless."

"I saw her drink two cups too many."

"No wonder she stumbled."

"Perhaps she was meeting a man."

Their explanations came too quickly, too easily. I wondered if any of them were true. At the base of the steps, a dark stain marred the stone where her head must have struck. Unfortunately, I was not able to see her body. It had already been borne away. One slipper still lay, however, on the landing above, as though snatched off, either in struggle or flight.

I studied the stairs. No broken tread, no torn hem snagged on the railing. Nothing to suggest an accident. But caught between the stones, I spied a small white bead, its pale sheen dulled against the stone flags. I crouched and lifted it carefully, the cool weight delicate in my palm. It was a drop pearl, the kind that dangled from a golden clasp. I closed my fingers over it before anyone else noticed.

A myriad of questions made themselves known. Had Lady Margaret been careless, drunk, or had she been silenced? Why had she been on the back stairs at all? A tryst? A foolish errand? Or had she overheard something she ought never to have known? So many questions with no ready answers.

I thought of the venomous whispers that coiled through Whitehall, of the men bold enough to dream of a Queen's death. Lady Margaret had been young, ambitious, hungry for advancement. If she had overheard such talk, she might well have thought to profit from it. Blackmail, perhaps. A dangerous game—one she had lost.

As I rose from the steps, a shadow fell across me.

"You see it too." Hollingsworth stood a pace behind, his eyes narrowing as they flicked from the stair to my closed hand.

"This was no accident," I murmured.

"No." His voice was grim. "I don't believe it was."

He guided me away from the throng, down a narrow passage and into one of the long galleries where only the echo of our footsteps kept us company.

"Show me what you found," he said once we were alone.

I opened my palm, showing him the pearl. "It was torn from her earring. Look at the clasp—the gold is bent, twisted. Earrings do not simply fall away. Someone wrenched it free." I turned it in the light, my stomach tightening. "There are strands of her hair caught in it … and a trace of blood. She struggled."

He took it, turning the pearl in his fingers, his brow furrowed. "What do you know of her?"

I hesitated, then said, "She longed to be part of the Queen's inner circle and was eager to be noticed."

Hollingsworth's gaze sharpened. "Ambition can be perilous. She may have allowed that craving to guide her actions."

"What do you mean?"

"My friends tell me Lady Margaret kept company with Nathaniel Asquith. His circle has long been whispered against, their loyalty to the Crown in doubt." He closed his hand around the pearl. "If Margaret overheard more than she ought…or sought to use it for her advantage…"

"She was silenced to stop her from speaking."

He inclined his head. "I fear so." His gaze held mine, grave. "Have you spoken to the Queen? This may well herald an attempt against her life."

A shiver ran through me. "I meant to do it this morning, but—"

"You must not delay." His tone brooked no argument. "A life has already been taken. The Queen must know to guard herself."

I nodded, my resolve hardening. "I will speak to her today." A pause. "And afterward, I will inspect Lady Margaret's bedchamber."

His eyes widened. "You risk being discovered."

"It is worth the risk, if it leads to the truth."

A crooked smile touched his lips. "The last time you revealed who you were—where you came from—I only half believed you. But now? This confidence you bear? It was not there before."

Something in his look lingered, admiration unspoken yet plain in the curve of his smile, in the warmth that softened his dark eyes. For an instant, my breath caught. Lady Halloran might well fall in love with such a man. But I was not she. However handsome Hollingsworth might be, my heart belonged to Robert who grieved for me in my own time.

"Beware, Lady Halloran," he said softly. "They've killed once. They will not hesitate to kill again."

I could only nod.

Later that morning, I found Her Majesty in her private closet, a shaft of pale light falling across her as she bent over her prayers.

I sank into a curtsy. "Your Majesty, forgive my boldness, but I beg a word in private."

She dismissed her attendants, leaving behind only the soft scrape of a chair as the last woman withdrew. Once we were alone, Catherine gazed at me, her dark eyes steady. "Speak, Lady Halloran."

I hesitated but a moment before forcing out the words. "I fear for your safety. Lady Margaret's death was no accident."

Her brows drew together, but she did not interrupt.

"I beg you, ma'am. You must only take food and drink from those who came with you from Portugal, those you trust without question. And see that every dish and cup is watched from kitchen to table. There are whispers enough in Whitehall to chill the stoutest heart. I would not see them made truth."

For a long moment she was silent, her gaze searching mine. At last, she inclined her head. You are young ... but you know danger. Thank you. Your counsel—I will take."

Relief washed through me, tempered by fear of what was yet to come. "God preserve Your Majesty," I whispered.

Her faint smile held both sorrow and grace. "He must, if men will not."

She dismissed me and returned to her prayers, her lips moving in silence as candlelight flickered across her bowed head.

As I made my way from her cloister, the Queen's safety weighed on me. But heavier still lay the question that would not release its hold. Who had silenced Lady Margaret, and why? One place was bound to yield at least some of the truth—Lady Margaret's chambers.

CHAPTER 17

THE SILENT CHAMBER

*O*nce I left the Queen's chambers, Anne hurried to keep pace beside me, her skirts brushing the stone floor. "My lady, you cannot mean to—"

"I must," I cut her off in a low voice. "I must learn who silenced Lady Margaret."

She came to a sudden stop. "You believe she met foul play?"

"I do," I said, turning toward her. "Now tell me, where are her chambers?"

Anne hesitated but a moment. "At the far end of the west passage, overlooking the privy gardens. But, my lady, they will ask why you seek it."

I slipped a comb from my hair and showed it to her. "Let them ask. We will tell them that Lady Margaret borrowed this, and we've come to fetch it back. Doubt they'll question either you or me after that explanation."

She glanced down at the comb, weighing the lie. "And if they do?"

"We will smile and say it is my favorite, and I will not be parted from it." I offered the smallest of smiles. "Which is true enough."

Anne's gaze swept the corridor, measuring shadows and doorways with the instinct of one accustomed to moving unseen. "Very well. But you must not linger inside. If anyone should come—"

"I'll be quick," I promised. My pulse hammered, half with fear, half with anticipation. This was the step from which I could not turn back.

Anne gave the smallest of nods and moved ahead, her figure slight but purposeful as she made for the west passage. I let a handful of heartbeats pass, then followed at a distance, keeping to the fringe of light where the torches sputtered and the smoke gathered near the beams. The palace had a different sound now after Lady Margaret's tragic death—voices pitched low, steps cautious upon the rushes, the swift hush that fell when one drew near. In corners and along the walls, people formed uneasy clusters, breath and rumor mingling. *Accident* and *fall* drifted like gnats. *Murder* moved like a colder wind.

The west passage opened wide enough for four to walk abreast, its windows looking out upon the privy gardens where the yews stood clipped and still as watchmen. The air held a faint sweetness. A gardener had bruised mint somewhere below, and it rose cleanly through the stone's chill.

At the end of the passage, a door stood half a hand's width ajar, a strip of dimness in the light. Anne hovered there, head bent, listening. I held back as she slipped closer and murmured something low. A woman's voice answered, and in another moment, a woman emerged, arms full of linen.

Anne lingered only a heartbeat longer, then eased the door wider and flicked me an all-clear sign.

As I reached her, I asked under my breath, "Who was that?"

"The laundress," she murmured. "I told her my errand for your comb and asked if she had seen the chamber keeper. She had not. The room has not yet been set to rights."

"Good." It was the rare instance in which neglect served justice.

Anne pushed the door wider with the back of her hand, as though too respectful—or too wary—to touch the latch. "I will leave it slightly open and keep watch," she said. "If I hear steps, I shall cough."

"Two coughs for danger, one for time?"

She nodded once. "Go, my lady."

I slipped inside.

The air was close, neither freshened nor foul, but bearing that private scent that clings to a room whose owner has not yet risen. A breath of rose water, a thread of lavender, the powdery whisper of starch. The shutters stood partly drawn, admitting a slender band of pale light that lay across the bed and the floor like a silk ribbon. Dust motes turned lazily therein, indifferent to human tragedy. A pair of slippers waited neat and small beside the bed—no scuffs on the toes, no rushes clinging to the heels. The counterpane showed the shallow impression where a body had once lain and would lie no more.

A dressing table stood near the light, its surface an orderly scatter of a young woman's life—a pearl-handled brush, a few ribbons, the stub of a sealing wax stick, a tiny pomander. Beside them lay a book of hours with a pressed sprig of something pale trapped at the gutter.

I moved first to the hearth. Something about fire and ash will always draw the eye of any investigator. People burn what they wish to hide, and fire, when hurried, rarely finishes the meal. The grate held last night's embers, dulling to gray. I took the poker and prodded. A flake of black lifted and cracked, exposing a corner of paper no larger than a fingernail, browned and bubbled, with the ghost of ink crawling like a thin river across it. I bent close. Only the faintest curve of letters remained—*...quith*. It told me very little, but it did reveal someone had burned something recently. Otherwise, it would have gone up in smoke.

A single cough sounded from the corridor. Not danger—time. I needed to hurry.

I crossed to the bed, lifted the pillow, then the mattress edge. Met only dust and the forgotten safety pin of a lace. The trunk at the foot was locked. I traced the seam with my finger—no pry marks, no roughness. A prudent girl, then, or one who had cause to keep certain things close. I knelt beside the bed and peered beneath. A bandbox and a pair of pattens waited there. The bandbox contained a hat and veil, still faintly smelling of violets. Nothing else.

The dressing table called to me again—not the prettiness of it, but the whisper of order. A girl's vanity will reveal her habits. I slid open the top drawer and found neatly arranged pins, a coil of ribbon, and a sachet tied with blue thread. The middle drawer revealed quills, scraped to points with a careful hand, a knife that would do as well upon paper as upon fruit, and a little box of wafers for sealing letters.

In the back corner lay a scrap of paper cut close, no larger than a visiting card. Upon it, in a small, quick hand: *The garden stairs by the buttery, one hour after midnight.* It was signed N.A. Unfortunately, there was no date. But the ink was fresh enough to glisten where the pen had been lifted.

My blood chilled. More than likely, this summons had drawn Lady Margaret into the dark—and straight to her death. I slipped the scrap into my sleeve.

A second cough. Time again. Anne was urging me along.

The lowest drawer stuck. I tugged, and it yielded with a soft groan. At first glance, it appeared to hold only odds and ends, including a length of lace that wanted mending. But beneath the lace, my fingers found the edge of something firmer, wrapped in unbleached linen. I drew it out.

It was a book no larger than my hand, bound in brown leather worn soft at the corners, the strap cracked but whole. No name on the cover. When I lifted the strap, the leather sighed as though relieved of a burden. I flipped to the last pages where writing could be found. The last one bore no title—only a date written in a fine, even hand: *Anno Domini 1666, the 28th day of August*. The script was of its time—spidery, flourished—yet neat enough that I could make it out.

Footsteps swelled faintly in the passage. Not Anne's cough. But that distant tide that meant life was flowing nearer. One more glance would not hurt. I flipped to earlier pages and found: *"...dined with her Majesty in the lesser hall; Lady M— spoke too eagerly of a scheme that might profit those nimble of ear, and I thought her foolish for it. Sir E— stood with W — in the window embrasure; when I drew near they ceased their talk..."*

Here, perhaps, was all I had hoped for and more—a mind that had watched and recorded, a habit of putting into words what others left to air. I had no idea who the initials belonged to or if those conversations mattered at all. I blew out a sigh of frustration. It needed to be studied along with everything else. But not now. I had no more time to dawdle.

Just as I slipped the journal into the pocket sewn into my petticoat and let the skirt fall, an unwelcome sound reached me.

The click of the latch.

CHAPTER 18

A JOURNAL'S SECRETS

I went still, a hand to the back of the chair, a smile schooling itself upon my mouth even as my pulse leapt. The door moved a finger's breadth. Anne's shadow sliced the strip of light. She turned her head, eyes cutting toward someone behind her.

"Forgive me," she said, voice pitched for courtesy and ignorance at once. "My lady lent Lady Margaret a comb of tortoiseshell—the very one she favors for the evening curls. We came to fetch it back, if it please you."

A woman's voice answered—older, practical, neither hostile nor fond. "You'll find no combs worth keeping here. The chamber keeper is to clear it by noon."

"If we might look in the top drawer, mistress?" Anne ventured. "My lady is particular about the comb."

I slid open the top drawer loudly, lifted the comb I had earlier placed there to make our lie true, and raised my voice so the woman beyond might hear. "Here it is, Anne." I stepped into view, my expression arranged into mild impatience.

The woman at the door—broad-shouldered, with the rough hands of service—swept me a quick curtsy when she recognized me. "Beg pardon, my lady. I didn't know you were within."

"No harm done," I said. "Lady Margaret was known to me." Not precisely a lie. "I would not have her borrow my things to be thrown into a basket with the rest."

She bobbed her head again, a little abashed. "We'll treat what's left with respect, my lady."

"I expect no less." I let my gaze move across the room as though measuring nothing more than dust and disorder. "When will her effects be removed?"

"By noon, as I said. Her aunt has sent word."

"Very good." I turned to Anne. "We have what we came for. Thank you."

She caught my cue. "Yes, my lady." And to the woman: "Good day."

We slipped out, my fingers steady upon the comb, the book slipped into my pocket a small pressure against my side, as if it had a pulse of its own. The door to Lady Margaret's room closed, and I exhaled. Anne's eyes searched my face as we walked—a question there, and something like reproach, and behind both a fierce loyalty that would forgive me anything if it kept me alive.

"You should not have lingered so long," she whispered once we had put distance between ourselves and the west passage. "My heart nearly stopped when she approached."

"I know." I could not help the small laugh that escaped—thin, breathless, not at all like mirth. "But we have what we came for."

Her gaze dropped to my skirts, perhaps sensing that I had taken more than a comb. "What did you find?"

"A journal," I said softly. "Has to be hers."

"Lady Margaret's?" Her hand rose to her throat. "Sweet mercy."

"Hush." We passed a corner where two women stood, their heads bent together like pigeons, their whispers cooing and harsh by turns. "Not here."

We turned into a lesser passage, one the sunlight barely touched, where the panels had darkened to the color of wet walnut and the smell of beeswax hung heavier in the air. Here, the palace breathed more quietly. The servants who passed us kept their eyes low. A boy carrying a jug of ale stumbled in his haste and recovered, cheeks pink.

"In my chamber," I said, "I will read what I can. The hand is not impossible, but I will need a clear head."

"And if it names a man?" Anne's voice was almost not a voice at all.

"Then we will decide what must be done." I thought of Hollingsworth, the way his eyes had warmed when I spoke without flinching, the warning in his voice after. *Beware, Lady Halloran.* "I will show it to Hollingsworth."

Anne hesitated. "You trust him."

"I trust him to want what is right," I said, and heard the steadiness in my tone as if it belonged to another woman. "And I trust that he will not flinch from danger."

We reached my chamber without incident. Inside, I barred the door—not a habit here, but a necessity now—and drew the journal from my pocket. The leather left a faint bloom upon my palm, as if the oil from Margaret's hands still rose from it. I set it upon the table, where the light from the window fell best, and opened it to earlier pages than I'd already read.

Anno Domini 1666, the fifteenth of August. "*The King more merry than of late. Heard that Sir T— returned from Lambeth. N. A. spoke to me at last, but not of what I had hoped.*" The letters blurred a moment and then sharpened again. My eyes would need to learn the hand's little games. The next page carried more. *"Heard again the name Redwyke upon a whisper; advised by J— to keep my counsel and my ears open. Saw W— pass a paper to G.P., who stuffed it in his glove and walked as though his feet were sore."*

"G.P.," I murmured. "Gabriel Parquier?" The name leapt up from the well Hollingsworth had mentioned in the cloistered walk. If Margaret had noted him, then she had seen more than she should have.

A soft knock sounded at the door. Not the polite rap of a great lady, but the quick, economical signal of a man who could stand in plain sight and not be seen. I closed the book and slid it beneath the folded linen upon the table. Anne retreated to the far side of the room and busied herself with a basket as though we had never been more innocent.

"Who is it?" I asked.

"Hollingsworth." His voice came quietly through the panel. "May I enter?"

I lifted the bar and let him in. He entered as a man enters a sickroom—cleanly, without fuss, his gaze taking in the corners first, then the faces. He bowed to the courtesy that was due, but when he straightened, his eyes were all business.

"You have news?" I asked.

"I do," he answered. "Although it's not much, what I have may matter. Parquier has been abroad more often of late, holding quiet meetings. I have it from a man who watches doorways better than I do. And this—" He set upon the table a folded scrap, its seal broken. "Found where it should not have been. The hand is not his."

I opened it. The paper was thin, almost translucent, the ink hurried but deliberate.

The Swan Tavern. Midnight. No signature. No mark save a

faint smear, as though the writer had pressed too soon upon the wax.

"Whose hand is it?"

"A man who signs with an N and wears the Asquith crest," he said. "You see why I am uneasy."

Nathaniel Asquith. The initials found in Lady Margaret's journal.

My heart tightened. "He expects a meeting tonight."

"So it seems," Hollingsworth replied. "And if Parquier means to attend, then we may at last see the face behind the shadow."

"I have something also," I said.

I did not tell him at once. It was not coyness but the habit of a woman who has learned that once a thing is spoken, it cannot be recalled. I drew the journal out and set it between us, a small, quiet bomb.

He did not touch it at first. He read the shape of it as if the leather could speak. "Lady Margaret's?"

"I believe so."

He looked at me then, and for a moment the severity fell away and what remained was simple admiration—and worry. "You should not have done this alone."

"I was not alone," I said, thinking of Anne beyond the door. "And I am not now." A brief pause. "The initials N.A. are in it."

"Nathaniel Asquith, a younger son who makes up in zeal what he lacks in fortune."

"I believe that Lady Margaret had hopes in his direction."

His gaze sharpened. "You've discovered that much?"

"Yes, and I hope to discover more. But ... the handwriting is not what I'm used to. Initials, not names. They will be difficult to identify. I fear that time is not on our side." Not only for the Queen's sake, but my own. I needed to return to my own century.

His mouth tightened, not in displeasure but in calculation. "When you have read enough, we will keep the book in safer hands."

"Whose?"

"Mine," he said simply. "Unless you have another to suggest."

I shook my head. "No. Give me tonight. Tomorrow you may have it."

"As you wish." He inclined his head. "I must caution you to be wary, Lady Halloran. Your presence in the west passage was noted. They watch to see who grieves and who pries." His gaze flicked to the journal. "Do not give them cause to agree upon which one you are."

When he left, the room felt smaller for the knowledge he had brought with him. I opened the journal again and read on, lips shaping soundlessly. Lady Margaret's hand yielded, page by page, its secrets. She had been relentless in her watching. Had written names as a fisherman casts nets— broad, indiscriminate at first, then drawing tighter when she felt the tug of weight. Parquier. Asquith, Markham, Overton. Another note about the buttery stairs. She'd met Asquith there before. No wonder she hadn't thought twice about meeting him there again.

At the bottom of one page, barely inked, a line that made the skin at my nape rise: *"If I am wrong, I shall beg their pardon. If I am right, I will need friends."*

I closed the book and rested my palms upon it. "You have one," I said aloud, though she could not hear me. "I will not let you be the girl who fell in the dark without finding justice for you."

Anne turned from the basket then, her face composed but her eyes wet. "Will you go to him?" she asked softly.

"Hollingsworth? I will see him tomorrow and hand the

journal to him." I flipped the book back to the first page. "But first, I will copy what I can in case the original is taken."

"And then?"

"And then," I said, feeling the steadiness settle in me like a stone in a river, resisting the current, "I will find the man who pushed her into the dark and see that he steps into it himself."

Anne crossed herself. "God keep you, my lady."

"He had better," I said lightly, for her sake if not for mine. "I intend to be very troublesome."

CHAPTER 19

DECIPHERING A JOURNAL

*B*efore evening, the Queen sent notice that she was indisposed. So, thankfully, my services were not needed. I was grateful that the weight of ceremony did not press upon me. A quiet night was a rare mercy.

Anne left to fetch both our meals. Upon her return, she set down the tray upon the small table, careful not to rattle the dishes. "Cold meats, bread, and a bit of syllabub, my lady. The kitchens are in a flurry with the banquet, but I pressed them for something plain."

"Perfect," I said, though my appetite was small.

Anne bustled about in her quiet way, drawing the curtains tighter against the draught, setting my slippers nearer the fire. Her presence steadied me. She never pressed, never questioned overmuch, yet I always felt her sharp eyes missed little.

"Will you have me sit with you a while?" she asked when I pushed the food about my plate more than I ate.

"Yes. Mend if you like," I said. "I should read a little longer." Although I didn't know how much longer my eyesight would hold out. Candlelight did not provide the best illumination.

She perched upon her stool with her sewing basket, choosing a sleeve with a frayed cuff. The candlelight made a gentle halo around her bent head as she mended, her lips moving silently in prayer with each stitch. I set Lady Margaret's little journal upon the table and continued to make sense of the spidery hand.

The words swam at times, the ink thin and uneven, but I forced my eyes to follow the lines. Finally, I caught something vital. *Saw Nathaniel with the book again. He writes only initials. But they're easily deciphered by someone who knows his circle. Meeting dates, places, words spoken of actions to be taken against the Queen.*

I shivered. Margaret had not known the peril she courted, but I did. That little book—Asquith's ledger—had to be the same manuscript Merton had obtained. And the reason he'd been killed.

I tried to read more, but my eyes stung from the effort, the letters blurring into black scratches. I closed the book with a sigh. There would be no more reading tonight.

Anne looked up, concern on her face. "My lady? Are you ill?"

"No," I murmured. "Only weary. I believe I'll take to bed."

She helped me unlace my gown, her hands brisk but gentle, then folded it neatly across the chest. I stood in my shift, arms goose-pimpled in the chill, while she drew out a wrapper and laid it over my shoulders before tucking the coverlet about me.

"Rest well, my lady. I shall pray your dreams are kinder tonight."

"Thank you, Anne. Go on to your bed. I need nothing more."

She bobbed a curtsy, gathered her basket, and slipped away, leaving me alone with the fire.

The room fell still. Only the faint hiss of the embers remained, and the wind worrying at the shutters. I lay staring at the canopy, Margaret's words echoing: *actions to be taken against the Queen.* The phrase grew like a drumbeat in my mind.

I tossed upon the pillows, restless, until at last I rose again, wrapped myself in my robe, and drew the journal open once more. Candlelight spilled across the page, illuminating Margaret's small, slanted hand.

"...if I carry this to Her Majesty, my fortune is made. None but I can tell her, for none but I have seen it..."

I pressed my lips together. Ambitious to the last. She had courted advancement and found only death.

A soft knock broke the silence. Three taps, close together. My heart quickened. Doubted it would be Anne.

I went to the door barefoot, every board groaning. Hollingsworth stood in the shadows of the passage, his cloak hanging loose, the scent of smoke and ale clinging faintly to him. His hair was disordered, his eyes bright with fatigue and urgency.

"My lord," I whispered, pulling him quickly inside.

He gave a short bow, then cast a glance at the door as I barred it. "Forgive the hour. I have news, and little time."

"Sit," I said, motioning to the chair by the hearth. "Tell me."

He did not sit. He remained standing, one hand braced upon the chair back, the other still clenched in his cloak. "I followed Asquith and Parquier this evening. They left Whitehall after dusk, quietly, as though not wishing to be seen. I shadowed them to a tavern near Charing Cross—one not fit for courtiers, but they went in all the same."

I felt the blood drain from my face. "Alone?"

"No. Two others joined them. They sought a private room. Paid good coin for it. But they had a boy bring them food and ale. I paid him to relay what he heard. He brought me word enough." He paused, jaw tightening. "They spoke of the Queen. Of how she grows troublesome. And of Lady Margaret as well."

My breath caught. "What did they say of her?"

"That she had been a danger—that she had seen more than she should." He lowered his voice. "And they spoke of a book, one that belongs to Asquith. Kept for their own counsel. When Asquith spoke in his defense, Parquier silenced him with a look, but not before the words were plain."

I pressed a hand to my breast. "Margaret saw it. She was thinking about telling the Queen."

His gaze sharpened. "Show me."

I drew out Margaret's journal and laid it on the table. "Here. Written in her own hand. She wrote of seeing Asquith's ledger—initials, dates, words spoken. He kept track of it all for them. She thought it her fortune once she carried the knowledge to the Queen. Instead, it became her death."

Hollingsworth bent over the page, his brow furrowing as he traced the lines. "Ambitious, foolish girl. Yet not mistaken." He straightened, meeting my eyes. "This is why Margaret was silenced. She knew too much." He gazed at me for a long time before speaking again. "Tonight at the tavern. They also spoke of you, Lady Halloran. You have now taken her place in their suspicions. If they realize you know about this book—"

"I may meet the same fate as Margaret." The words broke from me before I could temper them. "We must find that ledger. It is the proof we need. Without it, Margaret is but a dead girl at the stairs, and Asquith, Parquier, and the other conspirators will still be free to weave treason."

He caught my wrist—not roughly but with force enough to stop me. "You will be cautious. Swear it. Promise me."

The warmth of his hand burned through the thin fabric of my sleeve. For an instant, I saw in his face not only warning but something unspoken—fear for me, yes, but also something more than that.

"I will be careful," I said even as my pulse quickened. "But I cannot be idle."

He released me, though his eyes lingered. "Then we will tread this dangerous road together. They have killed once. They will kill again."

I closed Margaret's journal with a snap, as if to bind the resolve within me, and handed it to him. "Then we had best move swiftly. They might hide their book. We need to find it before they do."

Hollingsworth inclined his head, half in respect, half in resignation, while he slipped the journal into his leather satchel. "We'll speak again tomorrow at the cloistered walk after we break our fast. Until then, bar your door. Trust no one but Anne."

"I shall."

A small grin rolled over his lips as he eased the door open. But as he slipped into the passage, a sudden burst of male voices rang out—courtiers returning late from the banquet, their laughter loud, their boots striking stone.

Hollingsworth froze. For the briefest instant, his eyes darted to my door, then to me, calculation flashing. Before I could so much as draw breath, he caught me by the wrist, spun me lightly against the doorframe, and pressed his mouth to mine.

The kiss was firm, practiced, calculated to hold attention —yet something in it set my pulse racing all the same. I felt the heat of his hand at the small of my back, the strength in his shoulders, the warmth of breath between us. The courtiers passed, chuckling, one calling some coarse jest about lovers at midnight.

When their voices faded, Hollingsworth eased back, his lips curving faintly, though his eyes still burned with urgency.

I pressed my fingers to my mouth, breath unsteady. "I am a married woman," I whispered fiercely.

"In your time," he murmured, voice low and rough with something that might have been laughter, or regret.

"In every time," I returned, though the words caught in my throat. I managed a shaky smile. "Although I must admit, you are a rather splendid kisser. The woman who wins your hand will be most fortunate indeed."

He chuckled softly, a sound half amusement, half resignation, then swept a bow with all the polish of a cavalier. Turning, he strode down the corridor, his cloak whispering against the stone, leaving me pressed against the door with my heart racing and a thousand dangerous thoughts tumbling through my mind.

CHAPTER 20

AN AUDIENCE WITH THE KING

Morning came pale and thin, a veil drawn over a restless night. The chapel bell had barely ceased its summons to morning prayers when I entered the cloistered walk, my breath clouding in the cool air.

Hollingsworth stood in the shadow of an arch, his face drawn, as though sleep had abandoned him. "Good morrow, Lady Halloran. I trust you have broken your fast."

"I have indeed. How fare you?" The shadows beneath his eyes betrayed him.

"I've known nights of better sleep," he admitted, voice low. Then his gaze hardened, a flicker of steel at last breaking through. "But my decision is made. Asquith's rooms must be searched, and I'll be the one to do it."

Much as I wanted to join him, that would not do. He would worry about my presence when he'd need to focus on the search alone. "How soon?"

"Tonight," he answered.

"Not earlier?" The matter was rather urgent.

He shook his head. "He comes and goes from his chambers while the sun shines in the sky. But he will be at supper with a naval friend. I've arranged for a key to his rooms and a candle that won't betray its smoke." A flicker of wryness touched his mouth. "If Providence favors fools and busybodies, perhaps She will favor me tonight."

I thought of the journal now in Hollingsworth's keeping, of the assignation note that had led Lady Margaret to her death, and of Merton's manuscript in my own time, which was no manuscript at all but a ledger of treason. "Be careful."

"That is the one thing I cannot be," he said. The moment came to an abrupt end when the Queen's steward appeared out of nowhere like a shadow that had learned to speak.

"Lady Halloran," he said. "Her Majesty requires you."

Hollingsworth's glance held mine for a heartbeat. "Let me know if her summons changes our path."

I inclined my head. After he melted away toward the inner court, I followed the steward through a hush of paneled corridors to a small closet near the Queen's privy chamber. Catherine of Braganza stood by a narrow window, hands laced at her waist, looking out on a sliver of garden already loud with sparrows. She turned when the door closed. There was worry behind her serenity, and something flintier beneath that.

"Yesterday ... you say I must watch what I eat, what I drink," the Queen said, her voice low but steady. "You say Lady Margaret—her death, no accident. You wish to know more." She lifted her hand, a quiet summons to honesty. "Now... tell me. What you find?"

Amazing how in her halting English she managed to convey so much with but a few words. However it was communicated, though, she was the Queen, and those were commands. "After Lady Margaret's death, I searched her chambers," I began. "The first thing I found was in the grate. Something had been burned there, though not completely. Only one fragment of writing remained—the letters '*...quith.*' I thought it might have been part of a name. *Asquith*, perhaps."

The Queen's gaze sharpened, though she said nothing.

"Then I came across a slip of paper. It was an assignation —'*by the stairs near the buttery*'—but with no date given. It was signed only *N.A.* Again, I thought of Nathaniel Asquith."

"Go on," the Queen said.

"Later, I discovered Lady Margaret's journal, hidden among her things. She saw Benedict Asquith's ledger. Although the book was filled with initials, she said they could easily be read by one who knew his circle. He recorded meeting dates, places, words spoken of action against Your Majesty. And she wrote…"—I steadied myself—"'*…if I carry this to Her Majesty, my fortune is made. None but I can tell her, for none but I have seen it…*'"

Her Majesty pressed her fingers together until the knuckles blanched.

"One set of initials was *G.P.*," I finished. "I believe that to be Gabriel Parquier. Alongside Nathaniel Asquith, they form the pattern Lady Margaret traced."

The Queen's voice was quiet, but it cut through the air. "The journal? You have it?"

Heat rose to my cheeks. "I… I thought it best to have someone keep it safe."

"Who?"

I faltered.

Her eyes narrowed, keen and shrewd. "Lord Hollingsworth?"

My surprise must have shown, for she allowed the faintest smile. "I have spies too. Those I trust. They tell me who speaks to my ladies." She paused, her gaze distant. "Lady

Margaret—she wish to marry Asquith. It bring her death." Her voice softened, almost breaking from its careful control. "Poor girl."

For a moment she stared past me, as if seeing Margaret's face still among us. Then her hands tightened, white at the knuckles, before she released them with sudden resolve. "We go to the King," she said. "You will speak."

"Your Majesty," I began, because it was not polite to contradict a queen, "I'm not—"

"You will speak," she repeated, gentle but firm. "The King hears my fears often. He is weary. He must hear the same words from another mouth. Come."

So we went. No procession, only the Queen, myself, and the steward walking at a pace that meant there would be no time for trembling. The King received us in an antechamber drowning in tapestry and light. His eyes quick and amused as if life were a diverting play and he'd had the good fortune to be seated in the front row.

"Madam," he said, and bent to kiss Catherine's hand. "So early. Ought I to be flattered or afraid?"

"Afraid," she said dryly. "But flattered is good. Lady Halloran will speak." She pointed a finger at him. "You listen."

His glance flicked to me. It was not cruel, only curious.

He stood in his shirtsleeves, the picture of careless ease, and I was struck—against my better judgment—by how very attractive he was. Charm seemed to rest upon him as naturally as breath. Little wonder women found it so easy to fall beneath his spell.

Given he was the king to command, I provided the skeleton of what I had told Catherine. I gave him every fact as I knew them. The ledger kept by Benjamin Asquith. The pattern of meetings. The pamphlets that called the Queen a Jezebel and worse. The name of Parquier placed over it all.

While I spoke, he paced. When I named men, he stopped. When I finished, he smiled with a softness that made me want to shake him.

"My dear Catherine," he said to his queen, "England breeds pamphlets the way spring breeds lambs. Half the realm calls you a saint and the other half calls you a witch depending on which dinner they wish to be invited to." He held up a hand to forestall her retort. "But—" The word hung there, careful. "Daggers are less amusing than dinner invitations."

Catherine's chin lifted a fraction. "She's not wrong, Carlos."

Carlos? His name in Portuguese. The intimacy of it startled me. Affection, even fondness, lay beneath the simple word. Curious, really, given his well-known fondness for other women. But then, kings and queens were not like ordinary couples. Different rules applied.

"No," he said, the playfulness fading from his eyes. "She is not." He turned to me again. "I will have Her Majesty's food and drink watched from kitchen to table. No plate to pass unattended, no cup without a loyal taster." He glanced at the steward. "See it done. Speak to May, the Queen's chamberlain, and to the Queen's own women."

The steward bowed and rushed out, no doubt to carry out the King's command.

"As for the names Lady Halloran has brought to us," the King went on, "I will make enquiries—quiet ones—of them as well as others." He ticked them off on inky fingers. "Overton. The little fish with sharp teeth who mistakes Parliament for a pulpit. The rest—Montagu, Coventry, Denham, Jermyn—are talkers born. They will whisper whichever way the weather sits. And Parquier—" He paused there, and even his smile admitted a draft. "Parquier fancies himself a builder of scaffolds. I should like to see him try to build one under my nose."

His lightheartedness irked me. "Your Majesty," I said, because I had not come this far to be gentle, "ladies die under noses every day if the men around them decide not to notice. Lady Margaret is dead. The ledger is proof. The men who wrote themselves into it intend to harm your Queen. This is not a cause to be taken lightly."

The King's look sharpened. "You argue well for a lady newly come to court," he said.

Too late I realized that, mild as it was, the reproof of the King's jest might cost me, and the Queen, dearly. And that would not do. "I didn't intend it as censure, Your Majesty, only as an observation."

Something like pride flickered across Catherine's face so fast I nearly missed it.

"Very well, Lady Halloran. Your *observation* has found favor with the King. I will put eyes where Parquier thinks there are none and ears where he thinks all are deaf. But if I find this is air only—"

"It is not," I said, and Catherine's hand came to rest, light as a blessing, on my arm. A caution. I'd said enough.

The King's humor returned like a cloak he shrugged back into. "Then let us not choke on our breakfast before we have it." He stepped close to Catherine and lowered his voice, not so low that I could not hear. "Be watchful. Indulge my precautions even when they annoy you. And, my dear heart, do not drink anything sweet that has not been sipped by a dull, loyal man first."

Catherine's mouth curved. "I will try to keep one or two dull, loyal men at hand."

"Between us," he said, glancing at me, "we may find three."

He dismissed us with a bow that managed to be both affectionate and kingly. Outside, the corridor felt colder.

Catherine walked a few paces in silence, then spoke without looking at me. "Thank you."

"I only said what was true."

"Truth is rare here." She stopped. "Tell your friend he is a fool if he travels alone."

She meant Hollingsworth. "He will not be alone," I said, and only after I'd said it did I realize I had decided for both of us.

Her gaze warmed by a single degree. "Then both be fools who live."

We parted there, and I retraced my steps through corridors that had acquired sharp edges. In my chamber, I found no peace—only a chair pulled back as if someone had risen in a hurry. Anne was not there. Odd. But then she probably had other tasks to do.

I wrote a note for Hollingsworth and sent it with a page Anne trusted to deliver it to him:

Met with the Queen who insisted on relaying the information to the King. His Majesty will have her table watched. He will inquire into our names. I will await word from you. But I intend to walk along with you.

The day stretched seemingly forever. Eager to do something, I walked through the garden to stand at the buttery stairs and measure how far a woman might fall if a hand caught her unawares. When the sun tipped and bled into evening, I was summoned to supper. With Anne still missing, I had to beg the help of another maid to help me dress.

Catherine's ladies placed me at her table, where their eyes measured everything I did. I ate because they pressed a trencher on me and watched me lift it to my mouth. I drank because a dull, loyal man sipped first and did not die. All the while I felt their glances slide toward me—polite, curious, watchful. Whether it was protection or suspicion, I could not tell.

When at last I was released to my chamber, I was surprised Anne had not returned. She'd been my shadow since I'd awakened in this time. But someone had lit the fire in the hearth. It had to have been her. Maybe she'd come and gone while I had been at supper.

On the table that lay in the center of the chamber I found a folded scrap sealed with a crest emblazoned with an "H". Had to be Hollingsworth's. I broke it open, heart quickening. The writing within was hurried but legible:

The ledger is gone, hidden. But there will be a meeting. Meet me at our usual place at eleven, so I can share what I know.

It was not poetry. But it was a plan.

I read the note twice, then tucked it with the others into the hidden pocket of my petticoat. The scraps from Margaret's grate, the assignation at the buttery stairs, a copy of her journal entries—all pressed close against me, like the steady beat of my heart.

When the bell spoke the hour, I gathered cloak and courage both. London held its breath. Something in the air tasted metallic, as if the city had a coin under its tongue.

"Live," the Queen had said.

I meant to. But before we earned the right to do so, we would more than likely follow a trail to a meeting to hear conspirators talk openly of treason.

CHAPTER 21

THE SWAN AT MIDNIGHT

London at midnight was never silent. Even within Whitehall's walls, I had come to expect mutters and stirrings, the cough of guardsmen, the restless whinny of horses in the mews. But once Hollingsworth and I left the palace precincts, the city's pulse grew louder, harsher. Alehouse songs staggered through shuttered windows. A cart rumbled down an alley too narrow for it, its wheels scraping stone. Somewhere a woman's laughter rose and snapped like cloth torn in half.

It had taken no small effort to persuade Hollingsworth to let me accompany him as he was certain we'd be discovered. While he seemed perfectly content to gamble with his own neck, he balked at risking mine. Only when I informed him that it was the Queen's express wish I join him that he gave way. But even then, he did it as though every step beside me were a personal trial.

I kept my cloak close, more to conceal the pounding of

my heart than to ward off the night air. Hollingsworth walked half a pace ahead, his stride precise, assured, as though the city itself admitted his right to pass unchallenged. He did not speak until we turned into a lane no wider than my arms' span, where the Thames' air thickened with tar and smoke.

"The Swan," he said simply, pointing straight ahead of us. "That's where they plan to meet."

The tavern loomed at the lane's end, its timber frame leaning toward the river as if conspiring with the tide. A crooked lantern swung above the door, its flame guttering against the damp breeze. Men pressed in and out without ceremony—sailors with their sea-stained coats, apprentices with caps askew, gentlemen cloaked too well for such a place but hungry for what could be bought in the shadows.

We did not enter by that press. Hollingsworth had arranged otherwise. A word to the ostler, a coin slipped neatly into the man's palm, and we were guided to a side stair half lost in darkness. It groaned under our tread, its bannister tacky with old ale. My nerves stung, every creak loud as thunder in my ears, but Hollingsworth's hand brushed mine briefly, steadying.

"Up," he murmured, and we climbed to the gallery.

From above, the Swan revealed itself as a hive of smoke and heat. The common room stretched wide, beams blackened by years of soot. Tallow candles guttered in their sconces, casting more shadow than light. Men crowded at tables, shoulders hunched, voices low, each gathering its own knot of secrecy. The air was thick with pipe smoke, roasted meat gone greasy, and the reek of unwashed bodies.

Hollingsworth leaned close, his breath warm at my ear. "Watch. See who commands, who listens."

I tried. My eyes skimmed faces I did not know—ruddy

seamen, powdered courtiers, ink-stained clerks. For a moment, I thought myself a fool for daring.

"That one," Hollingsworth murmured, so close his breath stirred the loose hair at my temple.

I followed his gaze.

"Gabriel Parquier," Hollingsworth whispered.

He'd entered without ceremony. His shoulders broad beneath a dark coat, his head lifted high, eyes sharp as steel under the lantern light. He took his place at a table where others drew near as if compelled.

"Denham," Hollingsworth whispered. "Montagu. Coventry. Jermyn." He pointed to each as he named them. "All bending toward him."

"Where is Asquith? I asked. "He should be here."

Hollingsworth's shrug was his only comment.

As I gazed back to the group of men, Anne's litany returned to me. They were wolves in human trim. And here they were, not whispering among themselves but gathering around Parquier, as if he were a sun they dared not turn from.

But suns do not remain in common rooms for long. After a scant exchange of papers and nods, Parquier rose. A boy hurried ahead with a candle, and the knot of men followed, vanishing up a set of narrow stairs at the back.

"Come," Hollingsworth murmured. His hand found mine, quick and sure, and drew me along the gallery. We passed through a passage no wider than a coffin lid, its beams sticky with age and smoke, until he shouldered open a smaller door. A broom closet, I thought, until he drew me against the far wall.

"Here." His finger pointed to a ragged hole, no larger than a shilling, through which a pale shaft of lamplight spilled. I pressed closer and found myself peering into a private chamber where the wolves had gathered.

Parquier spoke, his voice low but certain enough to carry. "This will do for our purpose. We do not wish for prying ears."

A chorus of male voices agreed, but a man near the hearth enquired, "Where's Asquith? He should be here." The very same question I had asked.

Parquier's gaze cut across the table, sharp as a blade. "He will not be joining us. He became a liability the moment he allowed Lady Margaret a glimpse of his ledger. A fool's mistake. He has been ... dealt with."

For a beat, no one spoke. Then Denham gave a short nod, satisfaction in the set of his mouth. Montagu let out a low chuckle, but it faltered halfway. Coventry shifted in his chair, eyes dropping to the floorboards as if measuring the distance to the door. Jermyn smoothed his sleeve with deliberate care, the gesture of a man reminding himself to appear unruffled.

The message was plain enough—if a gentleman of Asquith's standing could be struck from their number, so might any of them.

Footsteps creaked along the gallery behind us—light, practiced. They passed steadily enough until, just outside the closet, they faltered. Silence pooled there, heavy as breath held too long.

My skin prickled. Whoever it was had stopped. Listening. Knowing.

The pause stretched a moment too long. A low murmur followed—words I could not catch, directed not at us but at the door itself, as if the very timbers had betrayed our presence.

Hollingsworth shifted, quick as a blade drawn from its sheath. He cracked the door, head angled out into the smoke-thick air, and in one motion laid a coin down on the unseen tray. A finger to his lips. Quiet.

The tread belonged to a serving boy carrying a tray of

tankards. He hesitated, his gaze darting from Hollingsworth's face to mine, before lowering his eyes and moving on. Whether it was silence bought or merely delayed discovery, I could not tell.

I exhaled at last, my heart clattering like dice in a shaken cup.

On the other side of the peephole, Denham asked in a low voice, "Has the flame been set?"

My stomach plummeted. Flame? A figure of speech, or something more literal, more hideous. Dear God! Had they arranged for London to go up in flames? The Great London Fire had started September 2. Was today that day?

I dared not look at Hollingsworth, for fear my eyes would give me away. His hand, steady on the rail beside mine, brushed against my fingers—an anchor.

Parquier's lips thinned. "Set and struck. Pudding Lane's bakehouse flared but a half an hour past. Sparks are already jumping from roof to roof. The tenements are lighting up like torches." A slow, evil grin rolled across his lips. "By dawn, the city will be gossip and ash."

A man cleared his throat. "So the pamphlets were only noise to cover this?"

Parquier's smile was small and patient, as one explains arithmetic to a man who prefers numbers to conscience. "Pamphlets were the chorus. They stoked opinion, set the words to be picked up in market and alehouse alike. They were meant to take the people against the Queen. While they argued on paper, other things moved."

"What do you intend to do about the Queen?"

"The Queen and her entourage will flee Whitehall to where comfort promises protection," Parquier said. "Her jewels, her papers, her people—her passage will be as natural as any flight from flame. They will take to the Thames to flee from the fire. Men have been placed at the exits to Whitehall.

They will be misdirected to obscure passages and guided to boats of men who owe us favors. Once aboard, they will sail down the river, where the boat will sink with all aboard. In the chaos, no one will wonder at it. And we will finally have rid ourselves of a troublesome Queen."

Good heavens! They intended to murder the Queen and use the fire as their weapon.

A murmur of approval crept round the table. These men took pleasure in the neatness of consequences.

A voice—Jermyn's—cut through the hush. "The King knows of Asquith's ledger. Lady Halloran told him. Once Her Majesty falls, he will move heaven and earth to recover it."

"The ledger is gone, along with Asquith. It will never be found," Parquier replied, his tone blunt as a knife.

A lie. That very manuscript had survived the centuries—until Merton laid hands upon it.

"That is not our only concern, Parquier," Jermyn pressed. "Others have marked our whispers. Some hold the King's ear. Hollingsworth among them. He could easily point the finger at us."

"Then we shall discredit him," Parquier said coldly. "He is not as spotless as the King imagines. A skeleton here, a whisper there. Soon he will be undone."

I glanced at Hollingsworth. He gave the slightest shake of his head. I may not know him as well as I wished, but I would sooner trust him than the traitors gathered in the room.

"Would the King believe it?" someone ventured, as if policy might be polite in the mouth of a monarch.

"We will make our accusations loud and obvious," Parquier said. "Loud enough that the King will be counseled to remove Hollingsworth, not to demand proof. A throne can be shorn by rumor as swiftly as by sword—if the scissors move quickly."

Hollingsworth's grip on my sleeve tightened until his

knuckles whitened. I felt the anger in him at the casualness of his plotted ruin, but there was no comfort to be had. I needed to know the rest. Pressing my face to the rough plaster—the mortar tasting of dust and damp—I listened.

"How certain are you of your plans?" Coventry asked, skepticism threading his voice. "How sure are you that your men won't turn on us?"

"They've been paid well," Parquier replied, voice flat as stone. "They will not betray us. Should they try, they will pay for it with their lives."

"And if the King doesn't believe our accusations? What then?" Denham whispered.

Clearly, Denham was more concerned with saving his own skin than the plot against the Queen.

"Then some shall be sacrificed," Parquier said, his voice even. "A messenger who lied. A boatman who drank too much and told tales. A servant whose loyalty can be bought. A fallible chain always has a weak link." He shrugged as if he were merely discussing the weather.

My breath caught. Hollingsworth's jaw moved once, twice, but he said nothing. He did not need to. The plan, in all its ugly clarity, made speech unnecessary.

"We have heard enough," Hollingsworth breathed at last. His voice was a blade folded away. "Let us go."

"Hold!" a voice barked from within the chamber. "Who goes there?" The words cracked like a pistol shot. Parquier's head snapped up, his gaze cutting toward the very spot where we crouched. We'd been discovered.

We burst from the closet, tore through the gallery, and stumbled down the stairs until at last we spilled into the alley.

Outside, the city's breath had become a roar. Bells clamored in frantic warning as smoke coiled skyward, turning the heavens a furious orange. Panic-stricken crowds pressed toward the Thames—some clutching babes, others staggering beneath precious belongings. Not all would find refuge at the river. There wouldn't be enough boats for so many souls.

Those traitorous men had loosed the fire upon London—willing to raze homes, destroy livelihoods, and sacrifice thousands—merely to cloak their plot to murder the Queen.

"Halt!" A rough voice rang out. Parquier had stationed sentries at the exit.

We did not wait for a second command. My pulse thundered in my ears as we ran through the reeking alley, stones slick with slime. Hollingsworth's grip closed firm around my hand as we slipped past barrels and crates, until—after what felt an eternity—we emerged at last upon a quieter lane. Only then, certain no one followed, did we dare to stop to catch our breaths.

My voice came ragged, little more than a whisper. "They mean to kill the Queen and cloak it in fire."

"And burn down the city as well," Hollingsworth said grimly.

We had no time for more. We had to reach the Queen. So we ran, the fire at our backs, the smoke choking our lungs. London itself had become a pyre. With every stride, the fear gnawed deeper. We raced not toward salvation, but the ashes of a crown.

CHAPTER 22

EMBERS AT THE GATE

*L*ondon thrummed like a fever, its pulse quickened—uneven, dangerous. Hollingsworth pulled me through the narrow lanes, steering us away from the crush of bodies surging toward the river. Yet always he kept the Thames in sight, its damp breath drifting to us in cold draughts, guiding our course toward Whitehall. Every footfall rang too loudly against the stones, as though the city itself might betray us. From far off, bells clanged—the echo of a warning that had grown teeth.

He guided me around a heap of staves and a dog that warily watched with a single bright coin of an eye. We cut through a lane so tight the buildings leaned together like conspirators, their upper stories nearly touching. A woman leaned from one, hair in a long dark rope over her shoulder, and shouted at someone in a lower window. Their quarrel fell in fragments on us—*bucket... ladder... fool of a man—*

domestic, ordinary, and absurd against the shape the city was taking.

Smoke, I discovered, had a way of lying. It could mimic a hundred innocent things until it did not—tar at the wharf, pitch, a supper gone careless. But beneath them all ran a dry, bitter thread—old wood remembering a long, dry summer too well. That was what caught at the back of my throat now.

We reached a broader street where faces gleamed in the firelight—boys with bare heads and bright eyes, men forming bucket lines by instinct more than command. The first tongues of flame were not yet visible here, only a low wash of color bruising the clouds. Someone cried that it began near Pudding Lane. Another swore it was Farriner's bakehouse.

A knot of men came up the street at marching pace. Not the King's guard. Not the watch. Not the bewildered householders—too deliberate for that. Their coats were too fine, their hats pulled too low. I did not need Hollingsworth's tightened grip to know what he knew—Parquier's men. Had they found us or were they bound for some other evil?

We turned as though it were the most natural thing in the world and slipped into a cut-through that stank of fish guts and rain. The men passed within yards, their boots biting into the grit. One of them laughed softly, the kind of laugh that promised we will have what we came for.

We stood out badly. Among the humble folk we looked too fine, too easily marked. "Do they hunt us?" I breathed.

"Maybe." Hollingsworth scanned the alley, listening with his whole body. "But Whitehall is not far. Stay close."

Close meant close. The lanes twisted like rope laid down by a drunkard's hand, but Hollingsworth knew their tugs and turns. We slid between a cart horse and its load, ducked beneath a swinging fish sign, skirted a courtyard where wet sheets had been laid to catch sparks—sheets already glittering with embers like wicked stars.

The bells had found their rhythm at last. Not pretty. But then alarms were not meant to be.

"They should pull down the houses," Hollingsworth muttered. "Make a firebreak."

"They will," I said, "but not for four days. During that time, London will continue to burn."

He halted, staring. "How do you know this?"

"I learned it in my schoolroom. I had an excellent governess."

"Does the Queen die?"

"No. She lived. But we cannot count on that. Perhaps *we* are meant to save her."

He shook his head, only half believing me, though fear and doubt warred in his eyes.

Soon, we gained King Street. The air shifted as if it had lost its mind—drafts from a dozen directions, each harsh with soot. We joined a stream of people moving toward Whitehall—some brisk and tight-lipped, some already wild-eyed and wailing that the world was ending. A peddler kept up with us for half a dozen strides and tried to sell me pins. I very nearly bought a packet out of pure gratitude for the absurdity.

Hollingsworth's pace lengthened. My skirts were not made for speed. Neither were my lungs. He reached back, and I took his hand. It was an odd, practical intimacy—fingers closing, palms locking—and it stitched me to the night with something better than courage. We crossed a small square where a watchman stood on a stool to be taller, bellowing for leather buckets until he was scarlet and righteous. The people ignored him, because that is what people do when they have already decided upon their own particular salvation.

At last the gate to Whitehall stood in front of us. Not the grand processional one, but a side entry with a door that had learned to open to the right kinds of knocks.

"Here," Hollingsworth said. "Quickly."

The guard there was the yellow-bearded one with the cracked tooth—good-natured so long as one was on the right side of him. Tonight his face looked different—younger, almost, or perhaps simply peeled down to its worry. Hollingsworth spoke to him too low for me to hear. But the result was what mattered. We were allowed inside.

Whitehall had its own kind of smoke—beeswax, rushes, the perpetual grease of meat, old cloth, perfume. Tonight all of it sat under the new smell like a second skin gone loose and peeling. A clerk brushed past with an armful of papers, anxious as a hen. A boy ran, then skidded to a halt because a running boy will always be shouted at by someone, even when the world is burning.

"Lady Halloran." The voice came from behind me. I turned to find one of the Queen's Portuguese ladies, the pretty one with pearl drops. Her eyes had the calm of someone who had made up her mind. "You will come."

"I am going there," I said. "To Her Majesty."

She dipped her chin in approval, then spared Hollingsworth only a single, swift glance that managed to take the measure of him without practicing any impoliteness I could catch her at. "You also," she said to him. "A little way."

We went together, the lady leading as surely as if she had a thread tied to the Queen's hand. The corridors had the wrong kind of life in them—servants darting, courtiers moving in clusters like cautious fish. Enough people had heard the word *fire* to make speed, but they had not yet seen it to make a show of composure.

Catherine stood in her withdrawing room with two women at her elbows and a third kneeling on the floor before a small coffer where her jewels lay. Beside it, a sturdier strong box waited, its iron fittings dull in the lamplight—a chest meant not for ornament but for coin, deeds, and whatever could not be left behind.

She showed no fear, only resolve. And wore a practical gown, the silk chosen for how well it moved rather than how it shone. When she raised her head and saw me, the muscles at the corner of her mouth softened. I felt absurdly pleased that I had impressed a difficult teacher.

"You are here," she said. "Good." Her eyes touched Hollingsworth next, cool and reading. "You also."

"A moment in private, Your Majesty," I said.

"No time for private. Speak now." When I glanced at her Portuguese ladies, she said, "I trust them."

"We heard Parquier at the Swan Tavern," I said. "He set the fire as a cloak to harm Your Majesty." It felt strange to use titles in a room where one woman's pulse was at stake, but the habit of them is a strong thing.

Hollingsworth bowed with the precise degree of deference one uses when there is no time for more. "They mean to move against you while the city's eyes are elsewhere."

"Your Majesty," I said, because I could not. "We must not let them within reach. Their words named you. Their hatred was explicit."

"Carlos knows," she said. "He sends men." A beat. "He will send more."

Her English grew flatter when she was weighing consequences. I could see the work of it in the set of her jaw, the careful order she placed on every clause. She took my hand for a moment—quickly, as if the gesture embarrassed her—and then let it go. "You will stay near," she added. "Tonight."

I nodded. It was not a command I had intended to resist.

Hollingsworth's eyes slid to mine with a meaning I could not mistake: *You must be where I can find you.* For his strategy, for my safety, and perhaps for something he would never say aloud. There are times when a woman's independence is a matter of dignity. There are others when it is a matter of folly. I am not so foolish that I could never tell the difference.

The door opened without ceremony, and a man I recognized as one of the king's men put his head in. He had the flustered air of a person who has just retired a necessary lie. "Your Majesty, the King asks—if it please—he asks that Your Majesty's women assemble the small coffer and the strong box. The wind is ... shifting."

In other words, the fire was growing closer to Whitehall.

"The wind is trouble," Catherine said, as a humorless smile touched her mouth. Her glance went to her women. "The jewel chest and the strong box," she said simply. "Watched, always."

"Yes, madam," said the kneeling girl. Jewelry chests and strong boxes, like queens, do not travel with legs of their own. Still, the ritual mattered. They would be watched.

The gentleman bobbed and fled.

"Tell me again," she said to me, softer now that the room had emptied a little. "What he said. Word for word."

It was not a speech for civilized ears. "They know you will flee to the Thames. Men watch every exit from Whitehall. They will shepherd you toward hidden passages and barges crewed by traitors—boats that will be sent downriver and then sunk with all aboard. In that wash of water and flame, they will rid themselves of a troublesome Queen."

When I finished, she pressed her fingers together until the knuckles made neat white lozenges beneath the skin. Then she breathed out and looked to Hollingsworth. "You will watch for him. This Parquier. Vanity will draw him back to Whitehall. He will want to see his scheme unfold. You will bear witness. You will bring word."

Reluctance flickered in his eyes. I saw it as plainly as the set of his jaw. He longed to remain at her side, to stand between her and danger. But loyalty bound him tighter than desire. He bowed his head. "As Your Majesty commands."

There was no bravado in it—only duty, reluctant yet unyielding. And there are few promises graver than those spoken against a man's own heart.

He stepped back then, and the smallest, strangest thing happened. I did not want him to go. Vanity, nerves, common sense—name it what you like. But the corridors outside had teeth, and the city beyond them had found its flame. I wanted an anchor, and the anchor was a man who had the bad habit of showing up precisely where I needed him.

"Take care," I said, for the more tender sentence would not pass my throat.

He understood anyway. His hand lifted, warm and steady, cupping my cheek for the briefest breath of time. "You as well." And then he was gone.

Silence lingered. Catherine watched the door, then looked back at me. "You should marry him. He make fine husband."

Heat touched my cheeks. "Your Majesty is gracious," I said, bowing my head as duty required.

But inwardly I knew the truth. He would find a wife one day. That much was certain. But it would not be me.

Time divides in a crisis. It both runs and sticks. We packed jewels like prudent thieves. We sent for clearer water. We moved chairs that did not want to be moved and put papers into the right hands. And then we took them back out again because the right hands kept changing. Through it all, the bells beat on, sometimes many at once and sometimes a dreadful, single insistence like a finger tapping a tabletop.

I went to the window eager to see, God help me, the city's destruction.

From here London had always looked like an argument

that had never been resolved. Roofs arguing with roofs about how a skyline should be. Spires jabbing their fingers into one another's ribs. Alleys sulking. Tonight, the argument had been decided. Fire wrote its verdict in strokes of orange and black. It was no longer a bruise on the horizon. It was a crown—a jagged one, ugly as wrath.

Behind me, the Queen spoke in that plain, careful way of hers. "We go to river soon. Boats there. Carlos will send for us."

"Yes, madam," her woman said.

"Lady Halloran." One of the women at my shoulder—the pearl-drop girl—touched my sleeve. "You not well?"

"I'm fine." My voice came out steady, to my credit. "Only thinking." I did not add that I was thinking of the embers leaping as cats do, from roof to roof, and a wind that had a malice of its own when it found a city built of kindling.

I looked back at Catherine. She stood where I had left her, not small but contained. I was struck again by that inconvenient affection I had developed for her—a thing entirely unsuited to our stations and therefore probably true. She caught my look and tilted her head the merest degree, which, in her language, meant *we go on*.

"Yes," I said. She had not spoken aloud, still I heard her.

The door opened again, and this time it was May, the Queen's chamberlain, with his neat bow and his face turned sharper by worry. "Majesty. The King's men ask for your movement to the river. Now."

"Now," Catherine repeated, and the word had no falter in it. "We go."

We gathered what had been gathered. We put out two candles and left three burning because superstition is a comfort when nothing else is. We stepped into the corridor. The palace had changed while we stood still. It had become a throat filling with smoke, slowly but with purpose. I could feel the pull of it toward the doors.

As we went, I glanced once more through a high, arched casement. The crown of flame had slipped closer along the city's brow. The wind dragged its edge like a knife. I stared a moment too long—drawn, horrified—and in that instant a single orange spark lifted on the draft, sailed high, and vanished into the dark.

A city holds its breath before it screams. London was there now—mouth open, chest tight—waiting to see if the fire would claim the ultimate crown—Whitehall itself.

CHAPTER 23

THE CITY AFLAME

May, the Queen's chamberlain, moved ahead of us like a needle drawing thread, stitching a path toward the river. Behind him walked Her Majesty, steady despite the press and the peril, and I kept close at her side, watchful. Her women clustered around us—two staggering beneath the strong box, another pair burdened with the jewel coffer. Both at our backs and in front marched the King's men, steel at their sides, driving the crowd apart with shoulders and command.

Catherine did not hurry. She permitted the world to make haste around her and went at the pace of decisions. Her English held firm in the crush—fewer words than anyone else's and therefore stronger. "Keep close," she said, and her ladies closed as if she had gathered them with her hands.

Smoke thickened by degrees, a lesson in incremental disaster. One breath tasted domestic—tallow and rushes. The next snapped like a match to resin. Above us, the bells had crossed the line between alarm and endurance. They were simply sound, steady peals.

At the river door, wind barged in, rude as a drunk relation. Torches guttered. Men shouted to one another from barges made suddenly precious. The Thames could be a savior when it chose, or a witness with its hands in its sleeves. Tonight it looked undecided.

The King's men had done their part. Boats were nosing the bank, black hulls with white slivers of wake, their oars crossed like ribs. One of Charles's gentlemen—sleeves rolled, face streaked with soot and sweat, less peacock than mortal—bowed and reached for Catherine's arm. She gave it, not because she needed holding but because the ritual would steady him.

"Your Majesty," he said, and when he looked at me, he was only a man grateful for an extra pair of eyes. "Lady Halloran."

May counted heads under his breath, the reliable arithmetic of loyalty. "All," he said. "Go."

We swayed in a clutch at the water's edge, the Queen's women first, then the box, then Catherine herself, light-footed for a woman who had been taught to move only on polished floors. She set her slipper on the gunwale as if it were a question and then answered it with the other foot. The boat dipped and took her.

I should have followed. That had been the plan—such as plans can be when the city is chewing on its own tail. Hollingsworth would see the Queen safely away; I was to meet him once the barge had cast off. Simple. Clear.

But just as my foot lifted from the quay, movement caught at the edge of the torchlight—a slip of shadow cutting across the fiery scrum.

Not a shadow. A boy. The page I'd entrusted with Hollingsworth's message. His cap was flattened, his eyes too sharp for innocence. He threaded through the throng with the wiry ease of one born to alleys, ducking past elbows and skirts until he was near enough for me to see the grime upon his cheek. He went beyond me, paused, and turned. Our gazes met—only for an instant—but in that instant I felt the world tilt.

He jerked his chin toward the right—toward the edge of the privy garden, toward the smaller river gate where servants and errand boys came and went unseen.

"You have a message for me?" My voice came low, the noise of the river and shouting men pressing close around us. "From Hollingsworth?"

He shook his head. "Your maid. Anne. She's in danger."

For a heartbeat, the world stilled. The crackle of burning timber, the cries of frightened horses, even the slap of water against the hull—all dimmed beneath the thudding of my heart.

Anne. My Anne. Loyal, stubborn, foolishly brave. Had she been caught in the crush? Had she been taken?

Cold reason whispered it could be a trap. Parquier was clever enough for that. But another voice, louder, fiercer, rose above it. If she needed me, I must go.

"Where?"

He flicked a glance over his shoulder, uneasy. "Follow me."

"Lady Halloran!" May's voice rang out above the din. "You must board—now!"

"One moment," I said, though even as I spoke, I knew moments were a luxury none of us possessed.

The barge lurched against the current, timbers groaning, and the Queen stumbled. May caught her by the arm and steadied her. She looked to me then—not as a ruler to one who served her, but as a woman who saw, in another's eyes, both loyalty and affection.

"Lady Halloran!" the Queen cried, her voice breaking against the wind. "Come. Now."

I shook my head. "Your Majesty, you are safe. You will live."

She stared at me, startled—as though I had uttered not reassurance but prophecy. Which I hoped I had.

The river wind caught my cloak and flung it back. For a heartbeat, everything stilled—the crack of the flames, the shouting of men, even the creak of the oars. Catherine raised her hand, trembling, and I raised mine in answer. No more words passed between us, but understanding did. This was farewell. We would never see each other again.

The page tugged at my sleeve. "My lady, come. You must follow me."

Before I could think better of it, I did.

The garden path felt like stepping out of a loud room into the inside of my head. The noise fell back as if it had hit a wall. Only the river's slap and the confiding whisper of leaves arguing with smoke remained. Ahead, the boy darted through the ironwork of a side gate left on the latch. I followed before common sense could finish her indictment.

The little lane beyond hugged the palace wall—a service way for carts and careless secrets. The smoke pooled there, low and dense, as if fire were a tide and this was its eddy. At the far end, the boy paused, put two fingers to his lips, and let out a note that was nothing like a whistle and everything like a signal.

The hairs on my arms lifted. Was I walking into danger?

I should have turned back. I should have gone to the river, to safety, to the Queen. But Anne's name had lodged beneath my ribs like a thorn. If they had her—if she was hurt—how could I live knowing I had abandoned her?

He went on. I went after.

We came out into a crooked run where the city asserted

itself—no palace here, only London as it preferred to be when not being watched. A row of mean houses leaned together like old gossips; a cat, singed at the tail, shot past as if personally offended by the heat. The sky to the east had stopped pretending to be night. It wore an ugly brilliance, the color of oranges that never grew. Sparks came in flocks, stinging when they landed. Even the wind had lost its sense of direction, spinning wild with the smoke.

I caught the boy at the corner. "Where are we going?" I asked.

He jerked his chin toward a narrow doorway half-hidden by a sagging awning. "Here."

The door creaked when he pushed it open. The smell that met me was foul—sweat, rot, and something copper beneath. The boy stood aside, his face blank, as I stepped within.

"Anne?" My voice came thin, hardly my own. "Are you here?"

"Milady…" Her voice was a whisper, a ghost of itself.

There—at the far end of the single room, slumped against the wall. Her gown was torn, her hair tangled, and her arms bound cruelly behind her. Blood marked her mouth and temple. When she lifted her head, one eye was nearly swollen shut.

Whoever had done this to her, I swore they would pay. I took one step forward before I heard the scrape of a boot behind me.

And in that instant, I knew. The boy had led me into a trap—exactly where they wanted me to be.

I turned, every nerve alert.

He stepped from the shadows—a tall man in a dark coat, the edges of it ash-dusted. His cravat was loosened, as though civility itself had melted in the heat. Only his eyes remained cool.

Parquier.

"Lady Halloran." The name rolled from his tongue as if it amused him. "How good of you to come."

I tasted smoke and iron. "You have no business with my maid. Let her go."

He gave a small, elegant shrug. "Ah, unfortunately, she knows too much. Same as Lady Margaret."

"You murdered her."

"The girl had the misfortune to see what she should not. And you, I think, have read what you should not." His glance flicked toward my empty hands. "Where is it? The journal."

So that was it. The book. Different from the one that brought me to this time and place, but still—a book with secrets.

Before I could say anything, the boy shifted, uneasy.

Catching the motion, Parquier smiled faintly. "You have been paid, have you not? You may go." The boy fled without a word, the door slamming behind him.

I forced myself not to flinch. "You'll gain nothing by harming us. The Queen is safe. Whatever you meant to do, it's finished."

"Finished?" He laughed softly, a sound with no mirth. "Nothing is finished, my lady. The fire has given us new beginnings. Some men will burn, others will rise from the ashes." He took a step closer, the boards creaking beneath his boots. "You could rise with me. Give me the journal and walk away alive."

Anne moaned faintly. The tremor of her shoulders, the blood streaming down her face, worried me. If she didn't get help soon, she might not survive. I couldn't allow that to happen.

I drew myself up, though my heart was pounding hard enough to bruise my ribs. "You mistake me for a woman who bargains with traitors."

"Not traitors," he said smoothly. "Visionaries."

"Then your vision is hell itself."

His smile thinned. "Enough! Search her!" he barked to someone who'd slithered into the room behind me.

Before I could turn, heavy arms pinned my wrists and bound them with rough leather. The man who held me reeked of sweat, dirt, and sour ale; his breath was a hot, animal thing against my neck.

Turning me as if I were a parcel, he raked through my skirts, shoved his fingers into hidden folds, and prodded the seams of my bodice. My face burned—not from the fire but from humiliation and fury. When his fumbling hands came away empty, he spat as though at a dog.

"She hasn't got it," he grunted, his voice thick with disgust. "The bitch hides nothing."

Before Hollingsworth and I had left Whitehall, I'd secreted my pocket's contents in the chapel.

Another of Parquier's men—a smaller fellow with a piggish mouth—stepped forward and struck me across the cheek. Pain flared hot and white, and the taste of copper filled my mouth. I swayed but did not cry out.

"Tell him!" the brute hissed in my ear. "Tell him where it is, and you might keep your life."

I lifted my chin, blood and spit at the corner of my mouth, and met Parquier's cold, narrow gaze. "You will gain nothing by killing us," I said, though my voice felt small.

He gave a short, mirthless laugh. "But I will—unless you cooperate." His mouth curved in slow amusement. "Tell me where you've hidden Margaret's journal."

"Never."

"So be it." He reached into his coat. A gleam of steel flashed in the darkness.

"My Lady, you must speak!" Anne's weak voice cried out.

"If I do, he'll still kill us," I said. "At least this way, we die with honour."

Parquier flicked a hand, though he did not yet raise the weapon. He wanted confession—the satisfaction of bending a proud woman to his will. And, of course, he wanted the book—the one he did not yet have. Around us, the building groaned, timbers protesting, a beam creaking overhead.

"The fire comes, Parquier," I warned. "Soon it will consume this building—and you with it."

Something high in the rafters gave a thin, terrible crack—the sound of a joist giving way—and for an instant, every man in that wretched room froze. The air grew thick with the stench of burning leather and scorched wood. Parquier's two minions exchanged a glance, then edged toward the door.

Sparks drifted down like startled gnats. Parquier's eyes flicked upward, irritated rather than afraid. With his attention elsewhere, I worked loose the leather strap that bound me.

When only dust drifted from the rafters, Parquier's shoulders eased. The smirk returned, faint but unmistakable.

"I tire of your theatrics," he said softly. "Tell me—"

The roof, having had enough, gave way. A great beam crashed beyond the curtained window, as dust and embers rained down like fiery ash from a broken sky. Anne cried out, choking on the smoke. Parquier swore and stumbled back, shielding his face. His men fled like the vermin they were.

"Best follow them, Parquier," I called, "before the flames claim you."

Another ominous crack split the air. He hesitated only a heartbeat, then turned and ran.

I rushed to Anne, untied her hands, and hauled her upright. Together we staggered toward the door. But before we reached it, the building, having had enough, finally surrendered. One final groan—one last shudder—and it came crashing down around us. I pushed Anne through the doorway to safety.

I was not so fortunate.

A beam struck true.

The world tilted as spark-flocks wrote orange punctuation against the dark. The ground received me with the side of my face and then with everything else.

Somewhere, far away, bells beat the city's heart. Voices went tinny, then vanished. Water laughed along a bucket line. The Queen cried out in her own tongue.

And then there was nothing but the taste of ashes on my tongue, and the slow, creeping silence of the grave.

CHAPTER 24

THE JOURNEY HOME

I was floating ... somewhere. In the smoke? The fog? I felt lighter than air itself, unmoored, drifting without a sense of time or place. For a moment I thought I might dissolve altogether, scattered like ash upon the wind.

Sound reached me first—dull, distant, as though I were listening through thick walls. Murmurs, perhaps? A low rumble that might have been a man's voice? But it ebbed and flowed, fading before I could catch its meaning.

Then touch—a weight at my hand, firm and steady, tethering me. The more I drifted, the more I felt it. Warmth seeping into me, pulling me back from that endless haze.

Scents followed next. Not the acrid bite of fire and burning timber I expected, but something sharp, sterile, carbolic, as if I were standing in the bright white corridors of a hospital ward. The realization startled me. Had I survived, then?

I tried to open my eyes, but light pierced them like needles, so I closed them again, retreating to shadow. Still, the fog had thinned. The smoke that had seemed all-encompassing was giving way to shapes, impressions. A chair creaking faintly. The soft clink of glass.

And that hand. Always that hand, holding mine as though it alone might keep me tethered to the earth.

I let myself sink into that warmth, following it back toward the world. The fog curled and shifted, reluctant to release me, but the hand in mine tugged, insistent.

My lips were parched, my throat raw, as though I had swallowed soot. I tried to swallow, but even that small act felt monumental. A whisper escaped—no word, only a sound, a rasp of being.

The hand stirred. Fingers tightened around mine. A chair scraped softly.

I forced my lashes to part, and the world swam into being—uncertain, blurred at the edges. White walls loomed too bright. A window curtained against the sun. A tall bottle of liquid hung from a stand, glinting faintly as each drop fell, steady as a clock.

Beside me, a face.

It took me a moment to place him, for exhaustion and shadow had remade him into someone almost unrecognizable. His jaw was rough with days' growth, his hair disheveled, his clothes wrinkled and stained as though he had slept in them. Yet when his eyes found mine, the fog broke apart, and I knew.

Robert.

His face crumpled—relief, disbelief, the barest quiver of his mouth before he pressed my hand to his lips. "Catherine," he breathed, voice hoarse with sleeplessness. "Catherine."

Tears spilled unchecked down his unshaven cheeks. He bent over my free hand—for the other was bound to the needle and tube—and pressed his lips to it, trembling. The salt of his tears warmed my skin as much as the kiss itself.

I tried to speak, to ask, to reassure, but my throat scraped raw, each word rasping as though dragged over gravel. "What ... have you ... done ... to yourself?" The whisper barely reached my own ears.

Yet he heard.

A strangled laugh broke from him, wet and uneven. He shook his head, pressing my hand tighter against his lips. "Look who's speaking. Thank God you're speaking." His shoulders shuddered once, twice, before he mastered himself enough to lift his head. His eyes—red-rimmed, hollowed with sleeplessness—searched mine as if to make certain I would not vanish again.

His face blurred once more as my strength ebbed, though his hand remained firmly on mine, the single tether holding me in the here and now. My lids drooped despite my will. The fog beckoned, soft and irresistible.

"No, don't go," he whispered, urgent now. "Stay with me, Catherine."

But even as he spoke, I felt myself slipping. My fingers stirred weakly in his grasp, and the effort cost me what little breath I had.

Panic lit his face. He sprang from the chair, nearly upsetting it, and crossed the room in two strides. He flung the door wide, his cry carrying down the corridor. "Nurse! Doctor!" His voice, so often controlled, cracked on the words.

Almost at once, hurried footsteps approached. A nurse, brisk and efficient, swept to my side. Robert fell back, one hand still hovering near mine, unable to let go even as she shouldered him aside to do her work.

She took her time in assessing me, cool fingers lingering at my wrist before brushing my brow. Robert hovered at the edge of the bed, his hands gripping the cold metal rail, his knuckles stark against the white enamel. He resembled a man standing trial, braced for a verdict that might restore his world—or shatter it beyond repair.

Finally, when he could bear the silence no longer, Robert asked, "How is she?"

"Conscious," the nurse replied, her voice calm, almost gentle. "The pulse is weak but steady. Better than we might have hoped. It's a good sign, though the doctor must examine Lady Rutledge."

A man strode in, coat flaring, urgency in every line of his bearing. His gaze swept over me before settling on the nurse. "How is she?"

"Awake. Pulse weak, but steady. A good sign," she repeated crisply.

He nodded once, then turned to me. "I'm Doctor Spencer. How are you feeling?"

"Confused."

"Understandable. You've been in a coma for three days. Do I have your permission to examine you?"

A test. I could tell. "Please do." I was just as eager as Robert to learn the truth of my condition.

As the doctor drew closer, Robert left the foot of the bed and moved swiftly to the other side. His hand hovered above mine, as if to steady me should I falter.

Doctor Spencer's spectacles caught the light as he bent over me, tightening a cuff around my arm. The hiss and tick of the pump filled my ears. "Blood pressure holding," he murmured after a few minutes. Next came the stethoscope, cold against my chest. No verdict there. Then, more firmly: "Now, follow my finger, if you please."

A pale hand moved before my eyes. I tried, though the effort made the room tilt alarmingly.

"Good. Now, can you count backwards from ten?"

I wet my cracked lips. "Ten... nine... eight..." The numbers rasped out slowly, but they came.

"Excellent." He leaned closer, eyes intent behind his lenses. "What is your name?"

"Kitty." I corrected myself. "Catherine Worthington."

He appeared confused.

"Your title, darling," Robert prompted.

"Lady Rutledge."

"Excellent," Doctor Spencer said. "Now, tell me, what year is it?"

The question struck me like a blow. For an instant the smoke returned—thick and choking—and I saw fire, not walls and courtiers in velvet and lace, not nurses in white. My lips parted, but no sound emerged. *Nineteen—? Sixteen—?* Both answers clamored at once.

Robert's hand closed hard over mine, willing me toward the present.

I forced a whisper through my raw throat. "Nineteen... twenty-five."

The doctor's gaze sharpened, then softened with approval. "Very good. That will do for now." He straightened, nodding to the nurse. "She's weak, but she's come through the worst of it. The main thing is rest. She needs to be quiet to give her time to recuperate. Start her on a liquid diet, nurse. A nourishing broth will do."

"Yes, doctor." The nurse adjusted the blanket, her movements brisk but kind. "You hear that, Lady Rutledge? You're on the mend. But you must rest. No exertions now."

I scarcely heard her. My gaze clung to Robert. My poor darling was a shell of himself.

The doctor gave a last nod. "She'll do." With that, he and the nurse withdrew, the door closing softly behind them.

Robert's thumb brushed absently across my knuckles. His face, although pale, appeared steadier now that the doctor had pronounced me on the mend. At length, he drew a ragged breath.

"I must telephone your parents," he said, voice low but determined. "They've been beside themselves. They deserve to know you've opened your eyes."

He hesitated then, his gaze flicking to mine, as though asking if I had strength enough to bear even that small intrusion of the outside world.

I managed the faintest nod. "Of course." Mother and Father would be frantic. The thought of easing their torment, even by a little, steadied me.

A nurse entered with a tray. The aroma that drifted from it told me it was more than likely the broth the doctor had ordered.

Robert turned to her. "Would you stay with her while I telephone her parents?"

She gave him a soft smile. "Of course, Lord Rutledge."

"Thank you."

His grip on my hand tightened, as if reluctant to let me go even for that small errand. "I'll be but a moment," he promised, voice rough with the weight of sleepless days. He bent and pressed his lips once more to my hand, lingering there, before carefully easing his fingers free.

The room felt colder without him, though the blanket was snug. My lids drooped, the fog beckoning again, but this time it held no terror. I clung to the echo of his voice and let myself drift, knowing he would return.

CHAPTER 25

GETTING BACK TO NORMAL

The next morning, Doctor Spencer arrived in my hospital room, spectacles perched on the narrow bridge of his nose, his manner brisk as scrubbed tile. He examined me as he had the day before—fingers cool at my wrist, the cuff tightening about my arm, the stethoscope an icy coin against my chest. He asked the same questions in the same even tone—my name, the year, and asked me to follow his finger. My responses came more surely this time, though my head throbbed dully, and a slow fatigue dragged at my limbs.

Robert was expected any moment. He'd left late last night to get much-needed rest. But Mother and Father were here, sitting side by side near the window, their hands clasped so tightly the knuckles showed white. The sight unnerved me. I could not remember the last time I had seen them so worried. My siblings—Ned, Richard, Margaret—had been eager to visit, but the doctor had advised against it. Too much excitement might slow down my return to full health.

At length, the doctor straightened. "You are fortunate, Lady Rutledge," he said. "You suffered a severe concussion. The shock to your system precipitated the coma. But no bones were broken, and I've detected no lasting injury. Your pulse is strong now, your responses clear, and you have begun to take nourishment." His glance softened, the severity of his features easing. "You may go home today."

Mother's breath left her in a small sound, half-sob, half-laugh. Father crossed to the bed and patted my shoulder with uncharacteristic gentleness. "Thank God," he murmured.

Just then Robert entered the room, so achingly familiar in the guise of the man I had come to love. Though weariness still clung to him, he was freshly shaven, his clothes clean, and his smile suggested a steadier frame of mind. He came quickly to my side and brushed a kiss across my cheek.

"How are you feeling?"

"Much better. I can now count to twenty," I teased.

That lopsided grin I loved made an appearance. "Progress indeed." He glanced at the doctor. "So what's the prognosis, Doctor Spencer?"

"Lady Rutledge can return home—on condition. Absolute rest for a fortnight at the very least. Bed, quiet, no excitements." He turned back to me. "Your head will ache. You may take aspirin, and if the pain becomes severe, a small dose of codeine. But only then. Nothing stronger, mind you. You may be sensitive to bright light and become easily tired. Do not push against it. Your body will mend itself if you allow it the peace to do so." He looked deliberately at Robert. "You must enforce these restrictions, Lord Rutledge."

"I shall," Robert said, his voice low but steady. "You have my word."

Doctor Spencer straightened. "A physician should look in on Lady Rutledge once she's home. Have you arranged for that?"

"Yes," Robert said at once. "I've already asked Dr. Larson to attend to her."

"Gerald Larson?" the doctor asked.

Robert nodded.

"He's an excellent physician. I'll leave word to make Lady Rutledge's records available to him." Doctor Spencer gave a satisfied nod and made a final note on his chart. "I'll send your discharge papers to the desk." And then he turned to me with a kindly half-smile, "You frightened your family, Lady Rutledge. Best not do so again."

"I shall endeavor to be perfectly tedious henceforth," I croaked, which won me a watery laugh from Mother and a look from Father that suggested even teasing would be rationed for the next fortnight.

After the doctor left, Mother kissed my brow. "My love," she whispered, her voice trembling, "If you wish to recuperate at Worthington House, you are more than welcome to do so. Your room lies ready, should you wish it."

"Thank you, Mother," I said, and meant it, though the idea of returning to my girlhood room made me feel both tender and somehow smaller than myself. "But I should like to go to my own home. With Robert."

Father cleared his throat. "Regardless, we shall accompany you to see you settled in. Your mother will not be denied that much."

Robert's hand found mine and gave the smallest, grateful squeeze. "Nor shall I," he said gently. "We will get you home as soon as we can."

It took more than an hour for the discharge papers to be processed. But by early afternoon, Robert's motorcar was rolling up to our Eaton Square address. As Robert helped me out, the air hit my face—crisp, clean, carrying with it the faintest scent of spring. So different from the sharp antiseptic tang of the hospital that tears sprang to my eyes.

The entire staff had assembled in the entrance hall: Mister Black, our butler, grave as a bishop, standing on his gamy leg; Mrs. Palmer, flour still ghosting her sleeves; several footmen and maids; Mister Hudson, Robert's valet; Mrs. Phillips, our temporary housekeeper and even little Elsie from the scullery, her gaze bright with relief, peeping from behind her. Their murmurs of "Welcome home, my lady," rose and fell like a benediction.

I tried to make a speech and could not. My throat closed on me. Instead, I nodded like a foolish queen and let them see the gratitude in my eyes. It seemed to satisfy them.

Robert guided me up the staircase, his arm firm beneath mine. He moved slowly, not because he needed to but because I did. He did not make a show of it. The steadiness of him—his clean, familiar scent, the brush of his sleeve against my hand—soothed something in me I had not known was raw.

Grace waited in my chamber, eyes shining. "My lady," she whispered, as if in church. "If we might ... this way." She guided me to the dressing room where, with soft hands and quiet efficiency, she eased me out of my day dress and into a soft lawn nightgown and robe. Then she helped me settle against cool linen that smelled faintly of lavender. The pillows cradled my head with a mercy the hospital ward had not known.

"Thank you, Grace," I said, and she bobbed a curtsy that was half a sob before whisking away to fetch broth.

Mother came and kissed me. Father patted my shoulder once more and promised to send flowers "only if the doctor approves of them." They withdrew with the tact they had learned when I married—reluctant to smother, determined to hover just out of sight.

Robert, thankfully, lingered.

He drew the coverlet up, tucking it around me with a care that made my throat sting. His fingers brushed a stray curl from my brow and stared at it for a long moment, as though memorizing its place lest I vanish when he looked up.

"I'm not going anywhere," I whispered. "Unless you move this pillow. Then I shall go to sleep at once."

His mouth twitched. "That is precisely where I wish you to go."

He sat on the edge of the bed and, after the briefest hesitation, kissed me, softly, gently. He captured my hand in both of his, as if he feared I might fray and float away.

I wanted to tell him everything. The smoke, the rush of heat, the roar of a city burning; the weight of velvet and the scrape of farthingales; the whisper of plots and a queen's steady eyes. But now was not the time. But sometime soon, it would be. I satisfied myself with that.

"We will talk tomorrow," he said, as if he had read my mind. "But today you rest." He leaned nearer and, with a tenderness that undid me, pressed a kiss to my temple. "Now go to sleep."

I fell asleep with his hand still folded around mine.

MORNING BROUGHT a pale light and a headache that throbbed behind my eyes. I had Grace bring me aspirin and a strong cup of coffee. Half an hour later, I was allowed scrambled eggs, toast, and marmalade. Breakfast had never tasted so good.

Doctor Larson, our family physician, called midmorning to check on me. Though he stopped short of declaring me fit as a fiddle, he was plainly satisfied.

"Remarkable, really, Lady Rutledge, that you've suffered no lasting damage."

"How do you explain it? As I recall, I was struck on the head."

"Your sturdy hat saved you from worse."

"I'll have to send a thank-you note to the designer. Perhaps they can use my endorsement to sell more hats."

He laughed. "I see your sense of humor hasn't been affected."

"Heaven forbid!"

Once he left, boredom set in. Robert had been called to a meeting at Scotland Yard, leaving me without his company. Grace brought fashion journals, but my eyesight soon tired. Doctor Spencer had warned me that it was likely to be affected.

Late morning, Grace attempted to read me a sentimental novel about a governess with improbable dimples. After the first chapter, I begged for a cup of tea with honey and lemon —something I never drank. But it took her away from me.

Once she went off to fetch it, I swung my legs over the side of the bed. The room tilted slightly. I waited until it steadied, then wrapped myself in my dressing gown, slipped on slippers, and slowly made my way along the corridor to my parlor, where a mountain of correspondence awaited me. That would have to wait. What I wanted was the telephone.

I asked the operator to connect me to the Ladies of Distinction Detective Agency. Doris, our receptionist, was startled to hear my voice. "Lady Rutledge! How are you?"

"As well as can be expected, Doris. May I speak to Lady Emma?"

"Of course." Seconds later, Emma's warm voice came on the line. "Kitty, how are you? We were so worried. I wanted to visit, but Robert advised against it."

The receiver was plucked neatly from my hand. Robert, my lord and master, had returned. "I apologize, Emma," Robert said, speaking into the mouthpiece, his tone clipped. "Catherine is under strict instructions to rest. So we must cut this conversation short. As soon as she's ready to receive visitors, I will telephone."

He replaced the receiver on the hook and frowned at me.

"I was bored," I protested.

"You're also white as a sheet. Come. Let's get you back to bed." He slid his arms beneath me, lifting me as though I weighed nothing, and carried me to our bedchamber where a red-faced Grace waited.

"Lady Rutledge is not to leave her bed again."

Grace bobbed a curtsy. "Yes, my lord."

"What if nature calls?" I muttered.

"Then Grace will help you to the lavatory. Otherwise, you stay put."

"You're being an ogre."

"Insults will get you nowhere," he said in a strict tone. But then his gaze softened slightly. "How are you feeling?"

"I'm fine."

He tilted his head, unconvinced.

"Very well," I admitted. "A little dizzy. My eyesight tires quickly. I can't focus for long."

"What can I do to help?"

"Talk to me. Tell me about your day."

While Grace left to fetch more dreaded broth and a sandwich, he pulled up a chair and obliged, recounting his interminable meeting at Scotland Yard. I meant to listen, but within minutes my eyelids drooped, and his voice faded into dreams.

Two days later, I was chomping at the bit. The headaches were now a dull thing, felt only occasionally. My eyesight had returned to normal—mostly. My energy was back—almost. I was now able to walk back and forth across my room unaided, with only minor dizzy spells. On the third day, I deemed myself ready to face the world. After my morning bath, I dressed with Grace's help and walked on my own to the morning room. I pushed open the door to find Robert at the table, a newspaper folded beside him, breakfast laid neatly to hand. He looked up, startled, then rose at once, crossing the room with his swift, economical stride.

"You shouldn't have walked here by yourself," he said, not unkindly, as he took my elbow and guided me to the chair next to his. "You could have fallen."

"I could have," I agreed, "but I didn't. And now, I shall have marmalade as my reward."

He gave me a look that would have cowed half of Scotland Yard. It had never done more than amuse me. As I let it wash over me, I busied myself buttering toast and ladling on marmalade.

"Would you like some eggs?" he asked.

"Yes, please, and bacon."

He approached the sideboard, ladled the food onto a plate, which he then placed in front of me.

"Coffee?"

I nodded. Once I'd taken a forkful of eggs and a slice of bacon, I asked, "How is the Merton investigation going?"

He put his cup down so forcefully I thought it might break. "No."

"No? What does that mean?"

"You are not to concern yourself with Merton's murder.

Not today, not tomorrow, not ever again. The doctor was explicit about you needing your rest. I will ensure you do so."

I set my fork down with care. "Robert, I lay for three days on that hospital bed. And now three more at home. I cannot just rest and sleep."

"You can, and you will," he said. It was the first time I had heard that tone directed at me—firm as a judge's gavel, not angry but immovable.

"Sweetheart," I said as gently as I could. "I need to know."

For a heartbeat, the air between us felt taut as a drawn wire. Then his gaze softened, the iron in his expression giving way to concern. He reached across the table, his fingers brushing mine. "I know how much it eats at you to sit idle," he said quietly. "But you've done more than enough. The case has been turned over to Inspector Simpson at Scotland Yard. He's competent. You can trust him to see it through."

Behind his gaze, I glimpsed the terror of those hours he spent by my side, not knowing whether I would live or die. The chair pulled close to my hospital bed. The steady drip of the glass bottle. His hand clasping mine as though sheer will alone might keep me tethered to the living. It was not a terror I could dismiss with a jest or a careless toss of the head. But he deserved the truth. It was time to come clean.

"I know how much you suffered," I said softly. "Not knowing if I would wake. Not knowing if I would live. Didn't you ever wonder where I was during those days?"

"On a hospital bed," he replied, his tone roughened by memory. "Unconscious."

"That's how it seemed to you. But in reality, I was not."

His brow furrowed. "Were you dreaming?"

"No. It was far too vivid for a dream." I paused, my pulse quickening. "I'd like to tell you where I truly was. May I?"

He hesitated, studying me as if weighing how much truth he could bear. Then he inclined his head once. "Tell me."

"You'll need to keep an open mind," I warned gently.

His jaw tightened, the faintest muscle twitch betraying his unease. At last, he nodded again. "I'll do my best."

I drew a breath to steady the tremor in my hands. "Then listen closely," I said, my voice barely above a whisper, "and I'll tell you where I truly was."

CHAPTER 26

THE TELLING

I told him slowly, because the telling dragged at something in me and sometimes haltingly, because the memory rose too bright, too close. I told him of awakening in another century, removed from everything I had ever known, discovering that I was one of the Queen's ladies, and not knowing how I was to go on. How my maid had helped me, how the Queen had trusted me, of her hand cool and steady, when I told her of plots against her, of the smoke that pressed like hands, of heat that breathed, of streets gone red and gold and black, the terrible knowledge that a city can be both hearth and pyre. I told him of the moment when both centuries clanged together in my skull, and how the only thing that brought me back was the weight of his hand on mine.

He listened without interruption, his face very still. When I faltered he poured more coffee for me. When I was finished, he said, "I think you should return to your bed."

"No, Robert. Not again. I need clarity. I need to find out what happened back then. But most of all, I need to find Merton's murderer in the here and now. Don't you see? They're both weaved from the same cloth."

"Catherine, all you had was a fevered dream. You somehow took the facts of that manuscript into your mind and created an entire story about what you had learned. That's all it was."

"I met Hollingsworth."

Robert blinked. "What?"

"Not our Hollingsworth, of course," I said quickly. "His ancestor—Edmund, the first marquis. I saw King Charles grant him the title with my own eyes, in the privy garden at Whitehall. I never knew that, Robert. Our Hollingsworth never once mentioned it."

When doubt flickered across his face, I pressed on. "Edmund became a true friend. We shared confidences, plotted how to expose the men conspiring against the Queen. At the Swan Tavern, we overheard their plans. They started the Great Fire to conceal their attempt to murder Her Majesty."

He studied me carefully, weighing my troubled expression, my worried gaze. "You're still there," he said quietly.

"Yes," I admitted. "When I close my eyes, I walk Whitehall's corridors again. In my dreams, I speak with Edmund, hear the conspirators whispering in the dark. Sleep brings no rest. It only carries me back. And until Merton's murderer is unmasked, I fear I shall never fully return to the present."

His hand closed over mine—strong, trembling, almost desperate. "God help me, Catherine, I cannot bear the thought of losing you again."

"You won't lose me," I whispered. "But I have to finish this. Only then will I truly come back to you."

He bowed his head, exhaling hard, then lifted his gaze to mine. "What do you propose?"

Relief swept through me. He was listening. And somehow, I had made him understand. "We convene the investigative committee," I said quickly. "I may not be strong enough to dash about London, but I can host the meetings here. I can charge the others with the legwork, set them to follow the clues. Together, we can unravel this knot without my collapsing in the street from the effort."

He regarded me for a long moment, the struggle written across his face. Duty warred with dread; love with the memory of the glass bottle dripping beside my bed. Then he rubbed a hand over his jaw and let out a faint, frayed laugh. "I can't believe I'm saying this."

"What?" Hope fluttered in my chest.

"You will only think," he said. "You'll do nothing more."

"It's the only work I can do," I replied, earning the ghost of a smile for my trouble.

He looked to the door, as if weighing the consequences of following through on what I'd suggested. After a while, he returned his gaze to me and nodded once, slow and grave. "Very well. We will meet in the library during which time you will remain seated. The meeting will last no more than an hour."

"That's not enough time." It would take most of that time to explain the circumstances surrounding Merton's murder, never mind my time in the seventeenth century.

"An hour and a half. That's my final offer."

"Fine." There was no use in arguing for more. He was determined.

His eyes sharpened. "You will rest beforehand. At least two hours in bed."

"Two?" When he frowned, I quickly said, "Fine."

"If you falter in the slightest—if your head swims, if your

vision blurs, if you so much as wince—I will end it then and there. Do you understand me?"

"I do," I said. "I accept your conditions."

His shoulders eased by a degree. "Tomorrow afternoon at three," he said. "I'll telephone everyone." He paused, then added softly, "Thank you."

"For what?"

"For giving me something less than terror to live with." He squeezed my hand. "Now, let's get you back to bed. If you are to play general from the library, you shall do it with your strength in hand."

I allowed him to help me rise. When the room tilted, he steadied me with a palm at my back. We stood for a moment —my head on his shoulder, his breath in my hair—before he guided me to the door with the care of a man carrying crystal through a crowded room.

In the corridor I glanced up at him. "Robert?"

"Yes?"

"If I falter, end it."

His mouth curved, not quite a smile. "If you falter, I shall carry you upstairs myself." He kissed my brow, then tucked my hand into his arm. "Come, Lady Rutledge. We have until tomorrow to behave."

I let him steer me toward my room, already counting backward through the hours: rest, meals, sleep, and then answers. Or at least the first tug at the knot.

CHAPTER 27

THE INVESTIGATIVE COMMITTEE

The following afternoon, under Robert's precise direction, the footmen transformed the library into a command post fit for an invalid investigator. A settee was drawn near the fire, a tray arranged before it with coffee and enough biscuits to satisfy a cavalry regiment. Robert oversaw every detail with military efficiency, then took his customary seat beside me—close enough to lend assistance should I so much as reach for a cup.

I watched his careful orchestration with mingled fondness and exasperation. No general ever marshaled his troops with greater vigilance. If he could have ordered the fire to burn more evenly for my comfort, I rather thought he would have tried.

"An hour and a half," he murmured as the mantel clock chimed a quarter to three. "Not a minute more."

"Then I will be thorough and quick," I replied, aiming for lightness. In truth, I was still a bit woozy, the world inclined to tilt if I moved too quickly. But I was not about to share *that* with him.

They came in twos and threes, trailing the day's rain behind them: Ned and Richard, crisp with purpose; Lady Emma and Lord Marlowe, radiating the peculiar serenity of the newly engaged, along with Lady Mellie, keen-eyed and brisk, as sharp and reliable as any ledger. The air smelled faintly of damp wool and city smoke, the sound of dripping umbrellas echoing faintly down the hall as Pritchard and the footmen bustled to take their coats.

As they entered the library, each pressed forward to ask after my health. To one and all, I gave the same answer. "Recuperating nicely, though not entirely out of the woods. And grateful to be here among family and friends."

Ned responded with his usual gravity, "And we're grateful to find you upright and lucid. Margaret and Sebastian send their love and good wishes. Oxford, and Baby Thomas, are keeping them quite busy." Although they'd intended to spend spring in London, their plans had changed, precipitating a removal to Oxford.

"I received a lovely letter from her conveying those same sentiments." As well as strict orders to rest.

Once everyone was settled and properly lubricated with tea, coffee, or something stronger, I folded my hands on my lap and proceeded with my rehearsed speech. "First of all, thank you for coming on such short notice. Second, I have been forbidden to do anything but think. So I will be counting on you to act as my inquiry agents—venturing out to gather information and bringing it back to this committee. I hope you don't find the tasks too onerous." I doubted any of them would object, but I had to mention it.

"I believe I speak for all of us," Emma said, "when I say we will do our very best to act in your stead."

"Thank you. I knew I could count on you." I took a deep

breath. "Now to get down to business. Robert and I will share what we know of Merton's murder. We will then decide as a group what steps need to be taken next."

"Shall I take notes?" Mellie already had pencil and paper in hand.

"Please."

Robert cleared his throat—his particular brand of warning. Keep it brief, keep it orderly, keep breathing. I inclined my head, and we began.

"Now for the facts," I started. Merton was struck down on London Bridge around sunrise several days ago. A deliveryman heard the cry and rushed over, but by the time he reached him, the assailant was gone. There were no other witnesses. Nothing was taken—his wallet, his watch, even his plain gold ring remained. That suggests theft was not the motive."

"Then what was?" Richard asked.

"You recall he mentioned a Stuart manuscript at supper," I said. "You were all there—you heard him speak of it. The next day I went to his shop to learn more. He boasted of its worth and hinted he would auction it soon. He claimed its contents could ruin a government minister once made public. Robert and I believe Merton was carrying the manuscript that morning. His killer struck not for profit, but to silence Merton. And to ensure the document never saw the light of day."

"So, a murderer and a thief," Emma said. After a pause, she added, "Where do we go from here?"

"Mrs. Merton contacted me the day her husband was murdered," I added. "She gave me two names—Sir Peregrine Loxley and Professor George Whitford. She said there was a third—a cabinet minister. But Merton never revealed his name."

"There was a fourth, darling," Robert said. "Monsieur Alphonse Duret, a French collector."

"Oh, yes. I'd forgotten about him."

"We need not worry about Monsieur Duret. He was in Paris the day Merton was murdered."

Ned frowned. "We have a dead man, a missing manuscript, and two names. Not much to go on."

I drew a long breath. "We have something more."

"What?" Richard asked.

"The past. 1666, to be exact." The date seemed to stir the very dust in the room.

Robert's hand shifted to cover mine. "Catherine—"

"I promised I would remain seated," I said mildly. "I did not promise I would remain in the present."

Their confused gazes found me. There was no more time. I needed to explain. Now.

"While I was ill, I dreamt. Not dreams of nonsense, but … a sequence. A place. London, 1666. Whitehall and the court of Charles II. I woke to find myself one of the Queen's ladies —Catherine of Braganza's own. I heard whispers, rumors, courtiers plotting to harm her. Upon further inquiry, I discovered two names: Nathaniel Asquith and Gabriel Parquier. Asquith was a scribe. He noted the details of the plot, and the initials of the participants, into a ledger. I believe that's the manuscript that Merton discovered."

No one spoke, and Robert did not interrupt. He only watched me with the kind of listening that feels like a hand at one's back. Mellie, whose imagination had always been practical, was busily writing down everything I said. Richard leaned forward, frowning, as if trying to reconcile the past with the present. Emma's lips parted slightly while her eyes went wide with the sort of astonishment she rarely betrayed. Even Marlowe, who wore skepticism as comfortably as his cravat, seemed briefly unsettled.

"I … befriended someone. He believed me, and together we investigated. Our search led us to the Swan Tavern, where we overheard the conspirators plotting treason. That same night, the Great Fire of London began. They had struck the match to cloak their scheme. My friend and I raced back to Whitehall to warn the Queen. She made it safely aboard a barge, but I … remained behind. My maid had been taken, and in my attempt to save her, I was struck down. When next I woke, I was in hospital with Robert at my side."

"Kitty," Emma said gently, concern written all over her face, "darling—"

"I know," I said. "A fever story. Smoke in a skull. I would gladly call it that if I could."

Ned let out a breath. "Suppose we accept—for the sake of argument—that your mind fetched this from somewhere. What are we to do with it now in 1925?"

"See where the echo lands," I said. "We have a murdered man in our day looking into this ledger from theirs. If Merton found a note, a reference, a family name—"

"—someone might believe he could stitch the two eras together," Mellie finished quietly. "And decided to cut the thread."

Robert spoke then, slowly, as though weighing each word. "Even if we grant the connection, we need facts from the here and now we can put our hands on. Who saw Merton last? Who knew he was asking about the ledger? Who benefits most from that book never being read again?"

"The families, I would say," Richard answered at once. "The ones with skeletons dating to Periwig Year."

"Some of those houses might be friends," Marlowe cautioned, glancing at Emma. "Or at least … acquaintances."

"If they are, we can use that connection to gain entry," Emma murmured, her tone brisk. "Doors open more easily to a friendly knock."

"So, where do we start?" Ned pressed.

"With Parquier and Asquith, two of the conspirators," I said without hesitation. "I talked to Sir Loxley and Professor Whitford. They could be interviewed again. Now that we have more information, we may be able to connect them to additional names—Denham, Montagu, Coventry, Jermyn. They were all present at the Swan Tavern plotting treason against the Queen."

The clock on the mantel ticked, solemn as a curate, each beat a warning that time was slipping through our hands. Rain tapped faintly at the windowpanes, as though London itself urged us on.

"Let's decide how to proceed," Robert said, ever practical, his voice carrying the edge of urgency.

The next half hour passed in quick debate, dividing responsibilities while I remained in my seat. Chairs scraped, voices overlapped, Mellie's pencil scratched furiously across papers. Richard and Marlowe argued over who ought to approach a certain peer, while Emma, unruffled, offered to smooth matters socially. Ned kept circling back to evidence —hard facts, verifiable witnesses—until Robert cut across the clamor and steered them back to order. At last, their assignments lay on the table, stark as a challenge. Robert studied them, then gave a single, short nod. "That will do. But it's only a beginning."

"A beginning is better than nothing, darling," I answered, though my pulse drummed with the knowledge that beginnings could not be delayed.

I could feel my strength ebbing. Our allotted time was nearly done, and soon I would return to bed, where I prayed my dreams might finally grant me ease. Robert, seeing my state, poured a cup of tea. Of course he did. Coffee would only keep me awake. His hand brushed my shoulder as he set the cup within reach.

Just then, the library door opened and a footman stepped inside. "My lord, my lady—you have a visitor."

"Hullo?" called a familiar voice from the threshold.

Hollingsworth.

He stood there, wind-ruffled, eyes alight with exhaustion, a ridiculous grin tugging at his mouth. For an instant, the room seemed to double. Two centuries sliding over one another like glass, Edmund's profile stamped upon his descendant's face—the same curve of the mouth, the same proud set of the shoulder.

My breath escaped in a small, startled sound as I lurched to my feet. The world tilted, my vision broke into light and shadow, and in the next moment I collapsed, fainting straight into Robert's arms.

CHAPTER 28

THE TERMS OF REST

The first thing I felt when I woke was the softness of linen beneath my cheek. The second was Robert's hand, warm and steady upon mine, as though he meant to tether me to this world lest I drift away.

When I opened my eyes, the familiar carved oak of the bedposts rose around me, solid and reassuring, their weight a sharp contrast to the memory that lingered. Hollingsworth's face—so uncannily like the one of his ancestor—haunted me. In the instant I saw him, the two centuries had collided, and I had balanced on the knife-edge of time.

"You fainted," Robert said quietly. His voice was measured, but the tautness about his mouth betrayed him. "I carried you upstairs. The doctor is on his way."

I tried for levity, though my throat felt parched. "It was merely the shock. You must not fuss."

"You call it fuss," he returned, his gaze fixed upon me with uncompromising intensity. "I call it nearly losing you before my very eyes."

I reached for his hand, squeezing it, partly to comfort him and partly to assure myself that I was, indeed, still here. "Do not bar me from the committee. They need my guidance. They need my knowledge."

"No, Catherine." The word fell like the gavel of a magistrate. "You will not return. The matter is ended."

Normally, I might have launched into protest. Instead, I found the strength leached from my limbs. My head still swam as though I were adrift at sea. Yet one thought burned brighter than all the rest. "Then at least ask Hollingsworth about his ancestor. I must know what became of Edmund Hollingsworth. He is the key, I am certain of it."

His brows drew together, a thundercloud gathering. "Catherine…"

"Promise me," I urged. Though my voice was faint, the urgency in it could not be mistaken.

For a long moment, he stared down at me, jaw clenched. At length he exhaled, resigned. "Very well. But only if you promise me this—you will rest. No tricks. No slipping back into the meeting. Rest and rest only."

I nodded solemnly. "I promise."

A moment later, a knock came and Grace ushered in Doctor Larson. He was as brisk as ever, spectacles sliding down the bridge of his nose as he crossed to my bedside.

"A fainting spell?" he asked, as though I were a schoolgirl guilty of malingering.

"Merely a trifle," I replied, attempting to sound airy.

But Robert snitched on me. "She was presiding over an investigative committee meeting."

The doctor froze, then fixed me with a look sharp enough to pierce a cuirass. "An investigation? In your condition?"

I sat up straighter, filled with indignation. "I am not an invalid, doctor."

"You will be, Lady Rutledge, if you continue in this fashion." He set his bag upon the night table and produced a stethoscope and then gestured me to sit forward. "Now—breathe."

I obeyed, if only to prove how hale and hearty I remained. He listened gravely, tapped my chest, and frowned as though my very lungs had offended him. And then he took my blood pressure with the dreaded cuff.

"Your lungs haven't been compromised, but your heart races still. And your blood pressure is a little high. You must allow yourself to recover, Lady Rutledge. Rest. Broths, teas, no stimulants. And above all, no more investigations for at least a few days."

I cast a glance at Robert, who looked altogether too satisfied. "It seems you and my husband are conspiring against me."

"Conspiring to preserve your health," he replied, tucking his instruments away.

When he had gone, Grace took up her post with all the zeal of a jailer. She brought broth upon a tray, scolded me for drinking too quickly, and fussed with pillows until I thought I might suffocate in goose down.

"Grace," I said firmly, when at last I could bear it no longer, "I am not an invalid. You need not stand guard at my bedside."

"But, my lady—"

"I promise to sleep. There, you see? I'm being a dutiful patient."

She looked unconvinced, but after smoothing the coverlet one last time, she withdrew. At last, I lay back, and—despite my intentions—drifted into slumber.

When next I opened my eyes, it was evening. The soft

light from a lamp the only illumination. My body felt steadier, though my mind leapt instantly to the questions that had tormented me. Edmund Hollingsworth. The Fire. The Queen.

Almost as if he'd sensed I'd awakened, Robert came through the door, his step purposeful, his expression unreadable.

"How are you feeling?" he asked.

"Well rested," I assured him, though my pulse had quickened at the sight of him. Could he have news? By the gleam in his eye, he did. "You know something."

He sat on the bed and gazed at me for a long time, measuring my breathing, no doubt, and the color in my cheeks. He must have been satisfied by what he saw because finally he said, "I spoke to Hollingsworth. About Edmund."

I forced myself to breathe normally. "And?"

"He survived the Great Fire and married Lady Halloran. They had three children—two sons and a daughter they named Catherine, after the Queen. He built the Hollingsworth estate that still stands today and lived long enough to see grandchildren."

I breathed out an easy breath. You couldn't ask more of life than that, especially in his age. But there was so much more I wanted to know. "What about the plot against the Queen? Were those traitors brought to justice?"

Robert hesitated, his gaze steady. "Richard telephoned Professor Whitford. He assured Richard there is nothing in the record. Although there were many whispers and rumors before the Great Fire, no actual plot was carried out."

I felt the blood drain from my face. How could that be? Had I imagined it all—spun from whole cloth by a mind too fevered with mystery? The Great Fire, the conspirators, the peril to Catherine of Braganza. Could it truly be nothing more than a mirage?

Robert sat upon the edge of the bed, his hand closing over mine once more. "Do not torment yourself. The past is fixed. Whatever dangers once loomed, they did not touch the Queen. After Charles's death, she returned to Portugal where she lived to the ripe old age of sixty-seven. Edmund thrived and sired a dynasty, our Hollingsworth and Mellie proof of that. That is what matters."

I turned my face away, unwilling to surrender so easily. In my bones I felt it. There had been a plot. If history recorded otherwise, then history had been deliberately smoothed, and the truth buried.

As though sensing the storm within me, Robert continued, "There is also news about the Merton investigation. Scotland Yard has a witness. A man who claims he saw Merton attacked."

My breath caught. "At last! And?"

"Unfortunately, the fellow is somewhat too fond of the bottle. His testimony is ... not exactly reliable."

"Still, it is something," I said fiercely, clutching at the thread of hope. "You must talk to him, Robert. Hear his account for yourself."

He looked unconvinced. "I dislike chasing phantoms."

"Not a phantom," I countered. "A man. A witness. However clouded his mind, he may recall something of value."

Robert hesitated, then inclined his head. "Very well. If only to silence your doubts. But you will not bother yourself with this."

I smiled faintly, recalling my earlier promise. "I have already agreed to rest. I shall keep my word."

That seemed to satisfy him, though his eyes remained wary. He bent, brushed his lips against mine, and murmured, "See that you do."

As he rose, I caught my tongue before the words could

escape. To tell him I meant to speak to Hollingsworth myself —whether in person or by telephone—would only provoke his disapproval and further restrictions. Best to let Robert believe I would remain docile, tucked up in pillows and the dreaded broth.

Robert lingered a moment longer, then turned and strode to the door. His shoulders were squared, the set of his back still rigid with concern. "I'll have Grace bring your supper."

"Not broth!"

He smiled. "Yes, broth, along with roast beef and potatoes."

I clutched my hands to my breast. "Be still my beating heart!"

He turned dead serious. "Don't."

Poor darling. He worried I would fade away again. "Not to worry, sweetheart. I mean to stay. If for no other reason than to find Merton's murderer." After a beat, I added, "And you. I missed you dreadfully while I was gone."

"Did you?"

"Of course, Robert. You're the love of my life."

The air grew still between us. "As you are to me."

Without another word, he withdrew, the door closing quietly behind him.

Alone once more, I sank against the pillows. Perhaps I had dreamt the danger of the past. Perhaps I had conjured Edmund's role out of desperation. And yet, deep within me, certainty pulsed like a second heartbeat: the truth had not been erased, merely concealed.

And when my strength returned, I would uncover it—whatever the cost.

CHAPTER 29

IN SEARCH OF EDMUND

*M*orning broke pale and uncertain, the sort of light that makes one question whether the world is truly awake or merely pretending. The curtains glowed with a soft haze, and the faint aroma of coffee drifted from the tray Grace had set beside my bed. My limbs still felt heavy, as though they belonged to some other creature entirely—but at least not as treacherous as they had the night before.

Robert had left for Scotland Yard before I awoke, his note left neatly upon the tray: *Remain in bed until my return*. The more he forbade, the more restless I became. There were things I needed to know. Things only Hollingsworth could answer. And that meant finding a telephone, the nearest of which was in my parlor.

Grace balked at the notion of my rising, but after a good deal of pleading—and perhaps a touch of quiet rebellion on my part—she relented, though only on the condition that she accompany me. So, with her hovering at my side, I made my slow progress toward my home office. The corridor was empty. Good. No witnesses to report my disobedience to their lord and master.

After locating Hollingsworth's number, I had the operator connect me.

"Hollingsworth House," came an impeccable voice. The butler, of course. He informed me that his master was not at home.

I had no choice but to leave a message. "This is Lady Rutledge. Kindly inform Lord Hollingsworth that I would be obliged if he would call on me at his earliest convenience." A mere telephone conversation would not suffice. I needed to see him.

Before Grace could properly scold me for my exertions, I allowed her to shepherd me back to bed.

An hour later, a discreet knock sounded. "My lady, you have a visitor—Lord Hollingsworth. He waits in the library."

My heart gave a treacherous leap. Finally, some answers. "Help me dress, Grace."

"Milady—" Panic flickered across her face.

"You may accompany me if it eases your mind. Hollingsworth can take over from there. Now fetch my dove-grey gown, if you please."

She clucked and fretted, muttering dire warnings all the while, but obeyed. Between us, we contrived a respectable appearance. She fetched my small pearls, insisting they lent me color. I allowed it. My complexion was rather pale.

Supported by her arm, I descended the stairs one careful step at a time. Twice, the world wavered, forcing me to grip the banister until the dizziness passed. Grace fussed like a broody hen, but I would not turn back. Pride—and sheer stubbornness—carried me downward.

As I entered the library, Hollingsworth rose at once. "Kitty, you look ... well."

"Lying was never one of your sins, Hollingsworth. I'm pale and still dizzy, but otherwise quite myself. My faculties are intact. And that's what matters."

After I settled into my favorite settee, I turned to my maid. "Thank you, Grace. That will be all."

"Yes, milady." She curtsied and withdrew, though not without a last, fretful glance in my direction.

"Coffee?" Hollingsworth asked, gesturing toward the silver service.

"Yes, please."

He poured with his usual care, adding cream and sugar before handing me the cup. "Now," he said, taking the armchair opposite, "what can I do for you?"

For one dizzying instant, the resemblance to his ancestor struck me so forcibly that the room tilted. Edmund's portrait —the proud set of the mouth, the thoughtful eyes that had seemed to follow me across centuries—was suddenly alive before me. I caught my breath, willed the weakness away, and steadied my hand on the cup.

Hollingsworth's brow furrowed, as if he had marked the moment, but he said nothing. He merely waited, patient and grave.

"Robert will have told you," I began, "of my—what he insists on calling—'fevered dreams.'"

"He did," Hollingsworth replied mildly, though curiosity gleamed behind his calm.

"They were not dreams." My voice emerged steadier than I felt. "They were real. Somehow—by what mechanism I cannot begin to explain—I slipped back in time and witnessed those days before the Great Fire. Your ancestor played a vital role."

He did not laugh or dismiss it as fancy. Instead, he

regarded me with that steady intelligence of his, fingers loosely cradling his cup. "You speak with remarkable certainty."

"Because it is the truth," I said firmly. "Tell me—did Edmund leave journals, letters, any record of his life? Something that might confirm what I saw?"

"I cannot say." Hollingsworth frowned in thought. "If such things exist, they'd be at Worthington Manor. The attics are filled with trunks and boxes my family hasn't touched in generations. I can telephone my estate manager and ask him to look."

Relief and hope surged together, bright enough to banish the last of my dizziness. "Yes, do. If anything remains in Edmund's own hand, it might illuminate what history has chosen to conceal."

"You have my word," he said simply.

I was about to thank him when the sound of the front door opening echoed down the hall. Moments later, Robert appeared in the library.

He halted on the threshold, taking in the scene—the steaming coffee, Hollingsworth opposite me, my unsteady poise on the settee. A frown flickered across his brow before he mastered it for our guest's sake.

"Hollingsworth," he greeted coolly. "Good to see you again."

"Likewise," Hollingsworth replied, offering no explanation, for which I was grateful.

Robert's gaze lingered on me. "How are you feeling?"

"Well enough to receive our visitor."

"That's good to hear," he said, though the doubt in his tone betrayed him.

He poured himself a cup of coffee and sat beside me. The familiar weight of his presence filled the room, as solid and grounding as the oak shelves surrounding us.

"How was Scotland Yard?" I asked.

"I spoke to the witness who saw the altercation between Merton and his killer."

My pulse quickened. "And?"

"He gave a detailed account," Robert said, his voice low and controlled. "Contrary to what Inspector Simpson implied, the man was lucid. He said he saw Merton shortly after sunrise, walking toward the southern end of London Bridge. Another gentleman suddenly appeared—tall, broad-shouldered, well-dressed, carrying a dark walking stick. They argued for several minutes. The witness couldn't hear the words, only the intensity. He moved closer. He was within a few feet when the stranger struck Merton with his cane. Merton fell, his head striking an iron piling. The witness said he'll never forget the sound."

A chill rippled through me. "And then?"

"The assailant bent over Merton," Robert continued grimly. "He rifled through his pockets, frantic, searching for something. Then he pulled out a small, leather-bound book. He described it as a merchant's ledger. The witness swears the man clutched it to his chest, looked around once, and vanished into the fog."

My breath caught. "The Stuart manuscript," I whispered. "The very account that was never meant to see the light of day."

Neither man contradicted me. The silence that followed was eloquent enough.

"When will the committee meet again?" I asked, steadying my voice.

"Tomorrow," Robert said.

I turned to Hollingsworth. "Will that be time enough for your estate manager to search the attics?"

"Attics?" Robert echoed.

"I asked Hollingsworth whether his ancestor left any

journals," I explained. "He believes there may be something stored at Worthington Manor."

Hollingsworth inclined his head. "I'll have him put as many hands on the task as necessary. If anything is there, we'll find it."

Robert addressed Hollingsworth, "You always did know how to rally the troops." They had both served in the Great War. Turning to me, he lowered his voice. "And you, my dear, should now be rallying your strength."

I met his eyes, refusing to yield. "Strength is precisely what I'm doing."

He sighed, exasperated but not unkind. "I suppose I should know better than to argue with you."

"Yes, darling," I said with a grin, "you really should."

CHAPTER 30

SECOND MEETING OF THE INVESTIGATIVE COMMITTEE

*B*y the following afternoon, I was quite done with resting. A single night's sleep had restored me more than a week abed ever could—well, that and the hope of answers from the journals unearthed in Hollingsworth's attics.

"You ought to remain in bed," Robert said over luncheon, arms folded like a magistrate delivering a sentence.

"I have rested quite enough," I told him. "I'll attend the meeting this afternoon, and that is the end of it. Unless you mean to carry me upstairs forcibly, you may as well accept it."

For a moment, he looked as though he might. Then he sighed. "Very well. But if you falter—"

"—You'll confine me to bed. I know. I won't."

"I'll be watching you."

"I should be disappointed if you weren't, Inspector," I said sweetly, hiding a smile behind my coffee cup.

When the hour came, we went into the library together. Grace lingered in the hall, ready to swoop should I stumble, but I managed perfectly well without her. Robert stayed close, his watchful gaze following me, though he made no attempt to usher me to the settee. He knew I needed to stand on my own—literally and figuratively.

Our company arrived on time: Ned and Richard, Lady Emma and Lord Marlowe, Mellie with her ever-present notebook, and Hollingsworth, composed as ever, as if no worldly disturbance could ruffle him. Coffee and tea steamed on the tray, accompanied by a mountain of biscuits and sandwiches.

Once everyone had settled, I stood, steady and sure, and smiled. "Before we begin, I must apologize for my fainting spell the other day. I assure you, it will not be repeated." At least, I fervently hoped not.

A murmur of polite laughter followed. Ned grunted approval, Emma arched a brow, and even Robert's mouth softened by a fraction.

"Now," I continued, "we meet today with more than speculation. We have new information, thanks to Robert's work at Scotland Yard. I'll let him explain."

Robert inclined his head and rose. "The inspector has located a witness," he began. "Not the most reliable fellow—fond of the bottle—but on this point, he was clear enough. He was on London Bridge at sunrise when he saw Merton quarreling with another man. He couldn't hear the words, but tempers were high.

"It ended quickly. The stranger struck Merton with his cane, and Merton went down at once. His head hit an iron piling. The witness swore the sound would haunt him forever. Then the stranger bent over him, searched his pockets like a man desperate for something, and pulled out a book. Small, leather-bound—the size of a ledger. He tucked it beneath his arm and vanished into the fog."

A heavy silence followed. Then Lady Emma spoke briskly. "But was this witness close enough to see the man clearly? Or is this all smoke and fog?"

Robert gave a single, firm nod. "He was close enough. He swore to the man's height—taller than most, broad in the shoulders. He noted a shock of red hair beneath the brim of a top hat. The cane wasn't merely carried—it was the weapon. Dark wood, silver knob. The blow didn't kill Merton; his head striking the piling did. It cracked his skull. That's the sound the witness remembers."

A stir went round the room. Mellie's pencil scratched furiously across her notebook. Richard leaned forward, eyes intent. Hollingsworth's gaze sharpened with thought.

I waited for the murmurs to fade before speaking. "Well then—a tall gentleman, red-haired, broad in the shoulders, carrying a silver-capped cane. Does that sound familiar to anyone?"

For a long moment, the only sound was the ticking of the mantel clock. Then Ned shifted in his chair, the movement abrupt enough to draw every eye.

"I know him," he said at last, voice low and reluctant. "Or at least I know a man who fits that description. Arthur Parker. I saw him often enough when I worked in the War Department. He was a junior minister then, always hovering where decisions were made. Hard to miss—tall as a lamp-post, shoulders like a boxer, and that hair." Ned grimaced. "Bright red, like a bloody flag. He always carried a cane too. Dark wood, silver knob. A ridiculous affectation at the time—though now…" He trailed off grimly.

Richard leaned forward. "Parker. He's in Cabinet now, isn't he?"

"Yes," Ned said. "Minister without Portfolio, last I heard. He's the sort who turns up everywhere—Trade, War Office, you name it. A man who makes sure he's in the room, whichever room it happens to be."

A heavy silence settled over us.

"Parker," Richard repeated slowly, tasting the name.

"Or perhaps," I said quietly, "Parquier."

The effect was instant—a ripple of shock, Mellie's pencil halting mid-stroke, Emma's eyes flashing.

"Names change easily when there's something to hide," I went on. "Parker is unremarkable enough to pass unnoticed. But Parquier? That name carries a history. And not one a man with ambition would want remembered."

Hollingsworth leaned forward, thoughtful. "If Parker truly is Parquier, the motive is clear. The ledger would tie him to his ancestor's treachery—proof enough to ruin a man who's built his career on respectability."

Robert's brow furrowed. "It's a leap. We can't condemn a man on a resemblance of names and a patch of red hair."

"No," I agreed evenly. "But it gives us direction. Merton died because he had that ledger. The man who killed him took it. And if Parker is Parquier, then the reason is plain—he couldn't allow the past to rise up and destroy him."

A murmur of unease rippled through the room.

"To prove the connection," I continued, "we'll need more than conjecture. Which is why I asked Hollingsworth to have his estate manager search the attics of his ancestral home. If Edmund left even a scrap of writing from those days, it might tell us how the ledger passed through the generations."

Hollingsworth's expression shifted, a flicker of amusement in his usually steady gaze. "My manager telephoned this morning. Although there were papers in the attics that dated back to that time, he suggested we should look elsewhere."

My brief hope faltered. "Look where?"

"The British Museum," he said.

A hot flare of irritation rose in me. Did he really need to add more mystery to our mystery? I had half a mind to seize Hollingsworth by the lapels. "Please explain."

He glanced briefly at Mellie, then back at me. "Years ago, our mother found a journal that belonged to Lord Edmund. A thick, leather-bound account of the Fire and the days surrounding it. She thought it of more value to scholarship than to family pride, so she donated it to the British Museum. Their rare books collection."

For a moment, I could only stare. "So it has been there all this time?"

He inclined his head. "Catalogued, cared for, but rarely touched. Because it's so valuable, only select scholars are permitted to view it."

Almost as one, we all turned toward Richard.

He held up his hands and laughed. "Don't look at me. I'm no expert on rare books."

"No," I said, smiling faintly, "but you are an Oxford man. And after the way the museum treated you, they should be eager to make amends. The new director, in particular, owes you that courtesy. You needn't check it out—only read it. If it contains names, records, anything of the plot, it could prove invaluable when this comes to trial."

Richard groaned. "You want me to go there now?"

"At the very least, arrange to see it," I replied. "There's a telephone in my parlor upstairs. You can speak privately there."

He muttered something about slave-driving sisters but rose nonetheless and left the room.

The rest of us took the opportunity to stretch. The ladies refreshed ourselves with tea and coffee; the gentlemen opted for whiskey. While we waited for the outcome of Richard's call, the conversation eased into a gentler rhythm—just like old times. Hollingsworth regaled us with tales from his travels—a misadventure in Greece involving a stubborn donkey and an overly enthusiastic guide, followed by a sunlit story of Mallorca that made us all dream briefly of turquoise seas instead of London fog.

Twenty minutes later, Richard reappeared, looking both triumphant and faintly resigned. He resumed his seat. "The director was delighted to assist. Special arrangements must be made to bring the book out from storage, so I'm to meet him at the museum in an hour. I'll be permitted to examine it, but only under supervision."

"Splendid," I said, clapping my hands lightly. "Then you'd best go before he changes his mind. Rare books have a way of slipping out of reach if one dallies."

Though Richard sighed, I caught the spark of curiosity in his eyes.

"Now then," I said, leaning forward once more, "let us return to the matter at hand. Ned, tell us more about Mr. Parker."

CHAPTER 31

THREADS CONVERGE

*A*t the close of yesterday's meeting, Robert telephoned Inspector Simpson to share our latest deductions—chief among them, that Sir Reginald Parker might very well be Merton's murderer. Explaining his reasoning proved a delicate task, as he could hardly mention my fevered dreams. Instead, he told the inspector that Merton had spoken of a cabinet minister's keen interest in the manuscript, and that the witness's description bore a striking resemblance to someone Ned knew. It was a tenuous lead, but persuasive enough for Simpson to pursue.

This morning, I awoke a different woman from the one who'd existed these past several days. My head was clear, my step steady, and my thoughts no longer shrouded in fog. When Robert gazed at me across the table from his bacon and eggs, he smiled with quiet approval.

After breakfast, he'd headed off to Scotland Yard to learn whether our lead had yielded anything of substance. With luck, he'd return in time for our investigative committee meeting. Everyone intended to be present—eager to hear both what Richard had uncovered in Edmund Hollingsworth's journal and what progress had been made in the official investigation.

By three o'clock, the library had assumed its now-familiar guise—half drawing room, half war chamber. The mahogany table gleamed beneath the afternoon light, its polished surface scattered with the genteel weapons of our campaign: sandwiches cut into neat triangles, a plate of delicate iced cakes, and silver pots filled with tea and coffee. At the far end, a decanter of whiskey caught the light in glints of amber fire.

I had barely settled in before the committee members began to arrive. Ned appeared first, followed by Lady Emma and Lord Marlowe. Hollingsworth and Mellie entered last.

"You look more like yourself today," Emma said, helping herself to a cup of tea.

"Feel more like myself," I answered with a smile.

"That's excellent," Ned said, visibly relieved. "Mother and Father have been quite worried. News of your improving health will do them a world of good."

"Please do tell them." I could only imagine how they must have suffered while I lay unconscious. Having lost a daughter to the Spanish flu, they would have been terrified of losing me as well.

"Any news from Richard?" Hollingsworth asked, pouring whiskey into a Glencairn glass for himself and another for Ned. It wasn't an idle question. Richard's research into his ancestor's journal had become the linchpin of our inquiry.

"No word yet," I said. "But even if he has no answers, he'll be here. He knows how eager we are for his report."

The atmosphere was far easier than at our first meeting. The stiffness had melted away, replaced by the easy familiarity of old friends drawn together by common purpose. Mellie already had her notebook open, pencil poised for duty. Emma and Lord Marlowe had claimed one of the settees, sitting bare inches apart—as affianced couples are wont to do.

I had just reached for my cup of coffee when the door opened and Richard entered at last, his satchel bulging at his side and his expression alight with triumph. He looked as though he had walked straight through the dust of centuries.

"I apologize for my delay," he said, brushing a bit of imagined soot from his sleeve, while he took his seat. "I wanted to verify something with Professor Whitford."

"You're only a few minutes late," I assured him, leaning forward eagerly. "So, what did you find?"

Even as I spoke, his hands were already at work, drawing several pages of close-written notes from the satchel and spreading them across the small table in front of him like prizes captured in battle.

"I had the privilege of reading Edmund Hollingsworth's journal—the record of our Hollingsworth and Mellie's ancestor," he began, his voice ringing with excitement. "It is no mere diary. It's a firsthand account of the Great Fire of London and of his role in bringing the conspirators to justice."

Mellie's pencil froze midair. "He wrote it down? Every detail?"

"Every important one," Richard said, eyes gleaming. "He described how he overheard the conspirators plotting at the Swan Tavern—just as Kitty said." He nodded toward me. "He recorded how he carried word to Whitehall, to both the Queen and the King. Her Majesty was moved to safety under royal guard, placed upon a barge with her ladies, and taken downstream before the flames reached Whitehall. He even noted that Lady Halloran assisted him, though he was discreet about the extent of her involvement."

"He likely wished to protect her reputation," I said, "in case the journal ever fell into other hands."

Emma leaned forward, her cheeks flushed. "So she was remembered, if only faintly. History may have blurred her name, but her presence endures."

"She did more than endure," Mellie said softly. "Thanks to her—and to Lord Edmund—Hollingsworth and I are here."

A shiver touched me, though I smiled to hide it. My small part in those long-ago events had not been lost entirely. Lady Halloran's name had survived, and through it, so had I.

"Did he mention the conspirators?" I asked.

"He did indeed." Richard unfolded another page with the flourish of a scholar, certain he held his audience fast. "Parquier vanished in the chaos, presumed drowned in the Thames. Asquith's body was found in the ruins, a victim of the flames—or so it was believed. The others were captured swiftly and met justice in short order. Edmund spared no detail—he recorded names, dates, and places with the precision of a man determined the truth should endure."

Ned gave a low whistle. "So the truth was always there, waiting in a dusty book no one thought to read until you pried it open."

"But none of this ever came to light," I said. "How can that be?"

"He explained that as well," Richard replied. "His Majesty did not wish the truth to become public. In the aftermath of the Great Fire, justice was quietly served, and the matter buried. Most believed the conspirators had perished in the flames, like Asquith. And, of course," he added with a faint, knowing smile, "no one questions a king."

The weight of Richard's words seemed to press the room

into silence. Then, with perfect timing, Robert appeared in the doorway and came straight toward me.

"Hello, darling." He bent to kiss my cheek. "How are you feeling?"

"Wonderful."

He studied me, as he always did, to confirm it for himself. Whatever he saw must have satisfied him, for he settled easily into the settee next to me. "So," he said lightly, "what did I miss?"

Richard offered a concise summary of his report. When he finished, I turned to Robert. "Your turn. Tell us what you learned at Scotland Yard."

"This morning," Robert began, "Parker was brought in for questioning by Inspector Simpson. While Simpson occupied him, officers searched both his home and his office. In the bottom drawer of his desk at home, they discovered a manuscript—a Stuart-era volume, seventeenth century."

"He kept it?" I asked. What a monumentally stupid thing to do.

"So it appears. Owing to its fragile condition, a rare books expert from the British Museum now has it in custody. Even from the brief passages he examined, there's an unmistakable reference to one Parquier."

The name rang through the room like a struck bell.

"A direct reference?" Hollingsworth asked.

"Direct enough," Robert replied. "And not only that—the witness who saw Merton struck down on London Bridge identified Parker as the assailant. Between his testimony, the Stuart manuscript, and Edmund Hollingsworth's account, there's sufficient evidence to charge Parker with murder."

I released the breath I hadn't realized I was holding. "Then it's done."

"Not done," Robert said softly, "but certainly begun. The Director of Public Prosecutions will review the evidence and determine the formal charge. Once laid before the court, Parker will stand trial for murder and answer for what he's done."

"Two manuscripts, from centuries ago, converging on the same name—and a witness to the attack," Mellie said. "It is more than enough." She turned to her brother. "And to think, our ancestor played a great part in it."

"Our ancestor—and Kitty," Hollingsworth said, gazing at me. "It's quite astounding."

Ned lifted his glass. "Well, here's to justice being meted out. He'll not wriggle free now."

The decanter caught the light as he poured for everyone, the amber liquid glowing like captured fire. I found myself thinking of another fire—the one that had nearly consumed a city, a queen, and, very nearly, myself.

Emma reached across and clasped my hand. "You have brought this circle to its close, Kitty. Without you—"

I shook my head, overwhelmed. "Without all of us. Without Richard's scholarship, Mellie's diligence, Ned's connections, and Robert's steady hand, never mind Lord Edmund's account. We are a chain—each link holding the others fast."

Robert's gaze met mine across the room, and I caught the faintest flicker of warmth. "Just so," he said.

The mantel clock chimed the quarter, breaking the hush. Glasses were refilled, sandwiches and biscuits eaten, and Mellie's notes folded into tidy stacks. Yet beneath the rustle and clink, a strange stillness held us all. We had threads enough to bind a man to justice—threads spun from fire and ash, from ink and paper, from courage and blood.

For the first time, I felt the weight of centuries settle upon me not as a burden, but as a mantle. The past had reached across the gulf of years, and we had answered the call.

CHAPTER 32

A MONTH LATER

ALL'S WELL THAT ENDS WELL

It was the first tranquil Sunday we'd enjoyed since the Merton inquiry. I was profoundly grateful for the return to Mother's beloved Sunday suppers. The windows of the Worthington House drawing room stood open to the mild May air, fragrant with lilac and the freshness of an earlier rain. The long table near the hearth—now cold, for we'd no need of fires in May—was covered with the remains of dessert: Mother's lemon-custard pudding, a bowl of sugared strawberries, a particularly scrumptious sponge cake, and the coffee and tea service.

In the weeks since Parker had been taken into custody, the case had moved steadily through official channels. Sufficient evidence had been found for the matter to be committed for trial at the next Assizes. With all that had been uncovered—the Stuart manuscript found in his possession, the witness statements, and, of course, Edmund

Hollingsworth's journal—Robert fully expected a guilty verdict.

"You're not too cold, dear, are you?" Mother asked. "A blanket can be fetched, or the windows closed if you prefer." She couldn't help but worry like a mother hen.

"Robert is keeping me quite warm," I assured her. Snuggled close to him as I was on the sofa, I honestly did not feel the least chill. "Thank you for offering."

"Very well. If you're sure."

"I am."

But even with that assurance, she spoke a soft word to our butler who swiftly moved to close the windows closest to me.

I glanced at the husband I adored, thankful beyond words for his love and steadfastness. The last month had not been without its difficulties. There were nights when the horrors of that house returned in my dreams—the smell of smoke, the creaking of timber, the fear. Each time, I would wake to find Robert beside me, ready to offer whatever comfort I required. Sometimes it was only his quiet presence; other times it took more to banish the ghosts. He always obliged, without hesitation or complaint.

Smiling, he whispered into my ear, "They're at it again."

"Who?"

He nodded toward the dessert table where Marlowe and Emma were arguing over the lemon pudding. Seemingly, there was only one bite left.

"You should give way to me. After all, I am soon to be your lord and master."

"Ah, but mine is the greater need. For I shall soon have to bear your pompous ways."

Ned soon entered the fray, his spoon poised like a judge's gavel. "Really, Marlowe, it's beneath a peer of the realm to squabble over pudding."

"I wasn't squabbling," Lord Marlowe replied, adopting an expression of wounded dignity. "I was defending my inheritance. Emma here has already taken two-thirds."

Emma gave a delicate sniff. "Two-thirds? A shocking exaggeration. And if you must know, I'm protecting what remains from your gluttony."

"Gluttony?" He looked around for allies. "You see how I'm spoken to by my own fiancée. It's tyranny in silk gloves."

Laughter rippled through the room. Even Father permitted himself a rumble of amusement behind his cup of coffee.

Mother set down the silver coffee pot with the air of a woman determined to restore order. "We can send for another pudding. There's plenty of custard in the kitchen."

"None of which he's getting," Emma declared, snatching the plate.

"That's hardly equitable," Marlowe said, lunging for it. "A man must stand for principle."

"Principle," she said sweetly, "weighs considerably less than your appetite."

The plate wobbled perilously between them until Mellie reached over, plucked it from their hands, and took the remaining bite for herself.

"There," she said, licking a trace of lemon from her spoon. "Problem solved."

The roar of laughter that followed nearly shook the chandeliers.

"Scandalous," Robert murmured beside me. "A theft committed in plain sight and no one calls for the police."

"Because we're all accessories after the fact," I whispered back.

Across the room, Hollingsworth raised his glass to Mellie in salute. She inclined her head with the satisfaction of a woman who'd just restored peace to Europe.

The conversation rolled on to safer topics. Ned and Lily's wedding arrangements. The weather in the Cotswolds. The latest news from Oxford. Richard had written that his lectures were well attended, though many of the students seemed more interested in King Tut's tomb than the trade routes that connected Egypt, Greece, and the Near East.

That earned another round of laughter. For a while I simply sat back and watched them—my family, my friends, all together, all safe. A month ago, that camaraderie had seemed impossibly distant, like something glimpsed in a dream. Now it was the most precious thing in the world, except for Robert, that is.

When the talk turned to wedding menus, I excused myself quietly and crossed to where Hollingsworth stood near the window. Evening light lingered over Grosvenor Square, turning the leaves of the plane trees to gold. The soft hum of motorcars along the square drifted in through the open windows, a steady heartbeat of London life.

"You're uncharacteristically quiet," I said to Hollingsworth.

He smiled faintly. "I was thinking how pleasant it is to hear laughter in this house. I missed it while I was gone."

I hesitated, then spoke the thought that had been troubling me since the night the case ended. "Hollingsworth, may I ask you something?"

"Of course."

"It's about Anne, the maid who tended to Lady Halloran." Even now, saying her name brought a pang. "I keep wondering if she lived through the Fire? I know it's foolish to care about someone who existed centuries ago, but—"

"It isn't foolish at all," he said gently. "You shared something extraordinary with her, even though I can't understand how it happened."

"Neither can I, to tell you the truth."

His gaze lingered on me, steady and thoughtful, a blend of fondness and something deeper—kindness touched with understanding. "I can't be certain," he said softly, "but I believe she survived."

My breath caught. "How did you reach that conclusion?"

He nodded. "There's a painting at Hollingsworth Manor—one I've passed a hundred times. It shows Edmund and his wife, the former Lady Halloran, with their children. Standing just behind them is another woman. I always assumed she was a governess. She bears a scar across her forehead and down her cheek. I thought it a strange choice for a portraitist to record such a mark, clearly a burn scar. But now I think I understand. It must have been her."

For a moment I could only stare at him. "Then she didn't perish in the Fire," I whispered.

"Apparently not. I didn't tell you before because I didn't want to give you false hope. After the Merton investigation ended, I traveled to Hollingsworth Manor. There were matters that required my attention. While I was there, I searched the attics myself. Among the old household records, I found mention of an Anne who cared for the younger children and remained with the family for many years."

I pressed a hand to my heart. "After all she endured, she found a home with them."

Hollingsworth's expression softened. "Apparently so."

The lump in my throat made speech difficult. "Thank you. I can't tell you how much that means to me."

He inclined his head in the way of a bow. "You've given her life, if only in memory. That's not a gift easily repaid."

From across the room, Mother called, "Kitty! Stop monopolizing Lord Hollingsworth and come advise us about the flowers. Lily insists upon roses, but I think she should carry lilies. What do you think?"

I turned back, smiling through the sting in my eyes. "I

think … it's the bride's decision to make. But maybe a compromise could be reached?" I suggested.

The room erupted in laughter once more.

Robert reached out a hand as I returned to my seat. "That was a wonderful solution. You sided with Lily, but did not completely disavow your mother's suggestion."

"She does love a wedding. And this will more than likely be the last one she'll help arrange. Well, at least for a while. I can't see Richard marrying anytime soon."

He studied me a second, his brown eyes perceptive. "You were speaking to Hollingsworth of the Fire."

"Not the Fire, of Anne. He believes she survived. There's a portrait at his manor that includes a woman with the family. Her face bears a scar."

Robert brought my hand to his lips for a kiss. "Then she was as resilient as you."

"I'll take that as a compliment."

"It was meant as one." He leaned closer, his voice roughened by feeling. "I know the past still finds you in the dark hours. But when it does, remember. I'll be there to steady you. Always."

For a moment I couldn't speak. The world, the room, even the ticking clock seemed to fall away until there was only his promise—and the quiet certainty that I would never face the darkness alone.

I let my gaze travel around the room—Emma and Marlowe sparring good-naturedly, as they so loved to do; Ned leaning close to whisper something that brought a blush to Lily's cheeks; Hollingsworth deep in conversation with his sister, while Mellie beamed, plainly delighted to have her brother home again. Mother, ever the perfect hostess, ringing for more pudding and coffee while Father watched her with quiet affection.

For the first time in weeks, I felt entirely content. Whatever ghosts the Fire had left behind, they seemed far away now. Not banished, exactly, but at peace.

Robert squeezed my hand. "What are you thinking?"

"That for once, I'm glad the world is perfectly ordinary."

He chuckled. "Don't get used to it. With you about, it never stays that way for long."

"Perhaps," I said, leaning against his shoulder, "but I can at least enjoy the illusion."

Outside, the bells of St. George's tolled the hour, their notes drifting softly through the open windows. A faint breeze stirred the curtains, carrying with it the scent of lilac and the distant hum of motorcars. London was alive—and at peace.

I let the laughter around me wash over me, feeling the last embers of that old fire fade at last. Whatever lay beyond this tranquil evening—mysteries, adventures, or weddings—I knew we would face it together, with Robert right by my side.

And that, I thought, was all the happily-ever-after I could ever wish for.

~

Did you enjoy *A Murder on London Bridge*? Then, you might want to take a peek at Kitty's next adventure, ***Murder at a Spring Wedding***.

Spring blossoms, wedding bells ... and murder?

Kitty and Robert travel to Wiltshire for the society wedding of the season, only to find themselves in the midst of another baffling crime when a guest is murdered at Hartleigh Hall. With a pompous local inspector bungling the investigation, Kitty and her merry band of sleuths must untangle family secrets, jealousies, and hidden motives before the killer strikes again.

Murder at a Spring Wedding, Book 14 in the Kitty Worthington Mysteries, promises readers a delightful escape into a world of 1920s glamour, country-house intrigue, and Kitty's signature blend of wit, courage, and charm.

CAST OF CHARACTERS

Kitty Worthington - Our sleuth

The Crawford Sinclair Family

Robert Crawford Sinclair - Kitty's Husband, a Scotland Yard Detective Chief Inspector. Recently inherited the Lord Rutledge marquissate title

The Crawford Sinclair Household

Pritchard - the under butler pressed into service when Mister Black breaks his leg
Grace Flanagan - Kitty's Lady's Maid

The Worthington Family

Mildred Worthington - Kitty's mother
Edward Worthington - Kitty's father
Ned Worthington - Kitty's oldest brother, engaged to Lady Lily Dalrymple

Richard Worthington - Kitty's next oldest brother

The Ladies of Distinction Detective Agency

Lady Emma Carlyle - Kitty's friend and partner in the Ladies of Distinction Detective Agency, engaged to Lord Marlowe

Lady Aurelia Holmes - Lady Detective

Owen Clapham - Gentleman Detective, former Scotland Yard detective inspector

Major Arthur Lane - Newest Gentleman Detective, Served in the Great War

Lady Melissande ("Mellie") - Assistant Lady Detective, and sister to Lord Hollingsworth

Betsy Robson - Bookkeeper, formerly Kitty's personal maid

Doris Perkins - Receptionist

The Wynchcombe Family

His Grace the Duke of Wynchcombe, Sebastian Dalrymple - married to Margaret, Kitty's sister

Her Grace the Duchess of Wynchcombe, Margaret Dalrymple - Kitty's older sister, now married to the Duke of Wynchcombe

Lady Lily Dalrymple - Sebastian's sister, engaged to Ned, Kitty's brother, currently living with the Worthington family

Baby Thomas - Sebastian and Margaret's son

Other Notable Characters

Oswald Merton, Shop Owner of Rutland & Merton, Antiquaries

Mrs. Margaret Merton

Lord Hollingsworth - A Marquis, Explorer and Adventurer and Robert Crawford Sinclair's best mate, traveling somewhere

Lord Marlowe - An Earl - Engaged to Lady Emma

Stuart Era Characters

His Royal Majesty, King Charles II
Her Royal Majesty, Queen Catherine of Braganza
Anne, Kitty's Maid
Gabriel Pasquier - Conspirator

This book is a work of fiction. All names, characters, locations, and incidents are products of the author's imagination, or have been used fictitiously. Any resemblance to actual persons living or dead, locales, or events is entirely coincidental.

Copyright © 2025 by Amalia Villalba

All rights reserved.

The uploading, scanning, and distribution of this book in any form or by any means—including but not limited to electronic, mechanical, photocopying, recording, or otherwise—without the permission of the copyright holder is illegal and punishable by law. Please purchase only authorized editions of this work, and do not participate in or encourage electronic piracy of copyrighted materials. Your support of the author's rights is appreciated.

ISBN-13: (EBook) 978-1-943321-46-9

ISBN-13: (Print) 978-1-943321-53-7

Hearts Afire Publishing

First Edition: October 2025